SKRITCH'S REVENGE

By:

Russell Nohelty

Edited by:

Esther Jones

Peter "Frog" Jones

Rhiannon Rhys-Jones

Lily Luchesi

Cover by:

Yoko Matsuoka

CHAPTER 1

Cats were supposed to have a wonderful sense of direction, and maybe they did because I was not a cat, no matter what people said about me. People tried to explain that fact to me every time I got lost, to which I responded, "I am not a cat. I am a cryptophage that resembles a cat, but I am not a cat." They were lucky I didn't rip their arms off with my cybernetic arm when they tried to give me scritches under the chin. Only my father, Jammer, could do that, and even then, only on his birthday.

"I wish you were a cat," Jammer growled into my earpiece as I backtracked down the air ducts of Gensys for the third time in the past ten minutes. "Then I wouldn't have to guide you like a child."

"If I were a cat, there's no way we would work together. I would be filled with the unflappable belief that I was better than you and present it outwardly at all times instead of just feeling it inside every bone in my body." I reached a four-way intersection just as the laser grid turned back toward my position. "Now, how about you show me a way that doesn't involve me being cut into a million little pieces, huh?"

"Fussy, fussy, fussy," Jammer said. "Okay, turn left. If you need to know which way that is, just hold up your hands and make an L with your thumb and index finger. The way where the capital L is facing the right way is left."

"Brilliant," I replied. "I have another finger for you. I'll let you use your imagination to figure out which one."

He was making a joke, but actually, it was helpful advice. Just because I was the size of a housecat didn't mean I was a cat. If I were a cat, I wouldn't have opposable thumbs, and the fact I did should have been a dead giveaway to anyone who saw me. I walked on two legs, I could talk, and I had both a cybernetic arm and leg, along with a metal exoskeleton running up my spine, and yet, every day, at least somebody mistakes me for one of those troublesome felines.

"Stop just ahead," Jammer said. "Wait for my signal."

"Copy," I replied, watching two laser grids crisscross each other.

Jammer was a dwarf, a thief, a hacker, and as close to a father as anything I had in this world. When my mother left me for dead after I was born with only one arm and one leg, Jammer took me in and made me whole again. He taught me how to walk, talk, hack, and steal; everything one needs to become a thriving child in an end-stage capitalistic nightmare hellscape like Zhakatal.

"Okay, get going," Jammer said after the laser grids swept by each other. "You have fourteen seconds before they make another pass."

I dug my cybernetic hand into the metal of the duct to get traction and leaped forward through the opening seconds before the laser grids passed behind me.

"How are you coming on disabling those grids? You know, the original plan before it all went to pot."

"Do you do anything besides complain? You have nanites. Why don't you do it?"

The most important thing Jammer did was teach me to use nanites. Only elves were supposed to be able to control the microscopic buggers, but our clan reverse-engineered them for ourselves. The elders originally didn't want me to have them, assuming I might be an elf spy, but after Jammer fixed me up and supercharged my brain, he contended that I was as much his kind as a cryptophage, and nobody fought him on it. Once I completed my cybernetic trials, they never said another word...to my face, at least.

"Because that's not part of the plan," I replied. "My part of the plan is sneaking through the grates and dropping the hacker disc into their system so The Spike can create a backend where they have access to their systems. You're the one sitting on your butt, supposedly shutting down the system so I can maneuver through these stupid grates in peace."

This was supposed to be a simple in-and-out job, a charity case, really. The Spike was a non-profit working to take down corrupt corporations, and it was something Jammer believed in wholeheartedly. There was a ton of corruption in Zhakatal, but gathering enough evidence was nearly impossible without a lot of help. If you could create a backend into the right server, you could make a mint reporting your findings to the government, but it wasn't easy. These companies locked up their systems tighter than a steel drum, and they became more sophisticated with every passing day.

I was less excited to work pro bono, but I was integral to the plan. Sneaking through grates wasn't something that a big, fat, husky dwarf could do. I was the perfect fit for all sorts of jobs like this one, which put our services in high demand throughout the city. I didn't have a head for computers, but I was pretty good in a pinch, and my ability to control nanites made me a commodity in the Bunghole, which was the area of the city where we lived. It was so named originally because the runoff from a local brewery made the whole place smell like stale beer. When the brewery closed, they redirected the sewer lines to feed out into the same tributary, and the Bunghole took on a different, but no less accurate, meaning.

"In fifteen seconds, take a right, an immediate left, and stop at the third grate," Jammer said after a few moments crawling forward. "Then you should be there."

I scuttled through the tunnels at Jammer's directions, avoiding another set of laser grids until I finally reached the grate. I peered through it to see an ancient computer that ran an obscure program Gensys needed to run the gyroscopics in one of their older model car engines. The system wasn't compatible with the rest of their security, but it was connected to their network, making it the single failsafe in an otherwise impenetrable fortress.

They planned to stop service on the engine model in three days, and once that happened, it would be impossible to hack into the system. No, it was now or never. As I waited for the technician to finish logging data into the system, a smirk crept across my face.

Bingo. Now, we play the waiting game.

CHAPTER 2

I nearly fell asleep watching the technician peck-type on the keyboard for an hour before, finally satisfied, they stood up and walked out of the room. The door closed with a thick seal, and a dozen lasers crisscrossed the room from different angles. They were stationary, unlike those in the ducts, though I still had to be on my A-game to navigate through them.

"I have a clear path inside," I muttered as I pressed my hands on the grate and allowed the nanites I kept inside my cybernetic arm to seep into the metal and loosen the bolts for me.

"Well, what are you waiting for?" Jammer growled back into my earpiece. "I'm not getting any younger."

The grate clicked as the nanites pulled it up into the duct with me. Then, they coalesced on the wall of the duct, creating a thin strand of rope for me to tie off my belt to allow me access to the room. It was the type of thing nobody else would even consider doing if they respected tradition at all. I figured tradition was what kept me on the outside looking in, and it could all burn down for all I cared.

"You're welcome to come in, old man, and show me how it's done."

"Don't get smart," Jammer replied, persnickety. "Remember who opens your cans of food."

He was the only one who could joke about me being a cat and get away with it, but he would pay for it later. I wasn't sure how, but I wouldn't allow his slight to go unpunished.

I pressed the nanites to a carabiner on my belt, and they clasped it tightly, just as they had done dozens of times before. When the "rope" was tight, I stood over the gap and fell forward until I was parallel to the floor. I spend a long moment adjusting to the position before kicking off the ledge and lowering myself down inch by inch.

It was slow going, and more than once, I had to crawl back up the rope and move along the ceiling to readjust myself. Even when I finally found a clear line to the computer, it took contorting myself in every direction to avoid the lasers with both my body and my rope. It was a dangerous dance. You could find the perfect hole through the lasers, but if your rope wasn't at the right angle, then it was all for naught, and you would alert everyone to your presence just because you didn't have the presence of mind to think before you acted. Thievery truly was more head than body, though you needed a bit of both to be successful.

Finally, after thirty minutes of slithering and snaking around, my foot touched the desk, and I pulled enough "rope" down to give myself some slack before skittering around to the front of the computer.

"I'm in," I said.

They gave us a schematic of the computer, and I used it to find the port that I needed to insert the disk. When it opened, I pressed the hacker disc into the computer before closing it again. The computer whirled to life, and for a moment, the laser flickered before a prompt came up on the computer asking for a password.

"Uhhh, we have a problem," I said as a countdown came onto the computer, ticking down from sixty. "Did you see a password in the schematics they sent?"

Jammer scoffed. "You would be so dead without me." There were several keystrokes, and with each one, the counter ticked down more and more as my heart pounded more and more. I could still get out if I went right now, but before I could consider it more carefully, Jammer's voice came over the earpiece. "It's $t1nky34."

"Really," I chuckled, but I didn't wait for him to confirm to type in the password. "That's what I call you."

"A password after my own heart."

"You can say that again, stinky," I chuckled. I pressed enter just as the countdown hit one. My heart jumped into my throat as I waited with bated breath. The computer flicked for a moment and then the screen went red, two dozen more lasers turned on, and a siren blared through the walls.

"Okay, maybe I don't have it."

CHAPTER 3

It was bad enough that three dozen new lasers appeared in an instant, but then they started to move, and that was even worse.

"Stand still, intruder. Our security system will deal with you promptly."

"What's happening, Skritch?" Jammer shouted. "Did everything go tits up in there?"

"That's not even half of how bad it is," I leaped between two lasers. Luckily, they were calibrated to cut through bigger fares than me, which gave me the ability to slide through the gaps between them, as long as I was careful. "Now, if you'll kindly shut up, I need to focus."

I kicked off the wall and leaped backward. I slid around another laser and held out my hand in the gap between life and death, beckoning for my nanites, but they did not come. *No, no, no, no, no. This was not good.*

I felt a burning on my shoulder and looked up to see the nanites raining down upon me, destroyed after their bodies touched the lasers. I had those bots since I was a child, and at that moment, I felt the crushing weight of every negative comment the elders made about me coming true, but there was no time to grieve unless I wanted to suffer the same fate.

Okay, Skritch. What's plan B?

As I pondered my next move, the door clicked open. The lasers dropped away, and a bulky hazmat suit waddled in, holding a blowtorch. They didn't say a word before lighting the whole room on fire. If I were any further from the door, I would have been scorched alive, but I was close enough to the door to avoid its blast, and I happened to be just small enough to evade the gaze of whoever was in the suit.

"Thanks!" I couldn't help but say as I slipped under their legs. "I thought I was a goner."

The sirens blared in sequence with the red lights flashing through the hallways. Half of the base seemed on high alert, scrambling for the exit, but the other half simply rolled their eyes and continued with their work. This must not have been the first time in recent memory the alarms blared, and I could use that to my advantage.

I slipped into a cubicle inhabited by a dead-eyed human worker just as a group of security guards made their way through the room. They craned their necks left and right but didn't find anything suspicious, so they moved on to the next cubicle. I peered around the corner as the security guards were getting an earful from the person in the Hazmat suit. They pointed toward my direction, and I pinned myself against the door.

"There's an entrance to the grate at the other side of the office." I looked up to see the dead-eyed drone speaking at me in a monotone. "Or there's a door over there, too, but you're just an itty-bitty thing. You don't seem big enough to open a door. Adorable, though."

"Listen!" I growled before thinking better of myself. I didn't like short jokes any more than cat jokes, but I decided to let it slide, taking a deep breath to calm myself. "Unfortunately, the grate has too many lasers, and I'm a bit too recognizable with the arm and leg to be mistaken for a house cat."

The drone stood up and put on a large trench coat that had, until that moment, been draped around the back of her chair. "Get in."

"Why would I—"

"And don't ask questions unless you want to get caught."

I didn't even take a beat to think about it before sliding into the coat as a security detail rushed through the halls toward our position.

"Where is that cat?" a security guard growled as they entered the room.

The others shrugged, and the dead-eyed drone did the same, except that they were standing. "I dunno. I'm just doing my work."

The security guard pointed to the coat. "And why are you wearing that coat? Take it off."

"Excuse me, sir, but it is cold outside, and that stupid alarm means we're supposed to evacuate. Now, are you going to let me go, or do I need to report you to the care team for a reprimand?"

"All of you should get out of here," the guard growled again, but it was clear, even from my disadvantageous vantage point, that the drone had won. "If you see something, say something."

She saluted him. "Yes, sir."

With that, the drone stepped out into the hallways as the guards split into many different directions. They buttoned their oversized coat so it wouldn't seem suspicious to have a bulge inside and then placed their hands inside the pockets to puff out the area around me.

"Why are you helping me?" I asked. "It's suicide."

"You're in trouble, and my mother taught me never to leave a man behind, or woman for that matter, if that's how you identify."

"I never much cared for labels," I replied. "Are you telling me you're a member of The Spike, the terrorist group that hired Jammer and me?"

"Yes, and why don't you broadcast it louder? It's bad enough my coat is talking, but there are ears everywhere."

"And eyes," I replied.

"The eyes I was able to take out before you slid into my cubicle. It's just the ears now, so shut up and let me work unless you want to spend your last few days in torturous agony."

I did not, so I took the advice and shut up, molding into the comfort of the coat. I would never admit it to any living being, but there were worse things than curling up in the pocket of a big coat with a warm human holding you pressed tightly against them.

I very rarely got the chance, as I had a reputation to keep up, but I did enjoy sleeping tucked into the blankets on Jammer's tummy. It was my happy place, and while I didn't so much like the blaring sirens, there was some comfort to be found in this person's warmth as well.

CHAPTER 4

I must have zoned out or dozed off because the next thing I remembered was two hands reaching into the coat and placing me on the ground. I was not too proud to admit I whined like a house cat when they jostled me awake.

"You should be safe now, little one." In the fluorescent light of the city, I saw my savior's eyes as not dead but a vibrant, shimmering window into a caring soul.

"Thank you," I replied. "What is your name, if I may ask?"

"It's best if you don't know. You can call me Mouse. I identify as she/her."

"That's not your real name, right?"

"It's my codename in The Spike. Real names are too dangerous, and I don't have a death wish."

I looked down at my arms, one now hollow without the nanites that used to be housed inside of it. "I'm not scared of giving my real name."

"No offense, little one, but we don't all have nanites at our beck and call." She looked down at me. "And some of us are too big to blend into the scenery."

"Is that a cat joke?" I bared my teeth at her. "Because if so—"

"Of course not. I'm not a monster. Who would ever be so dense as to call you a cat? That's offensive."

"You would be surprised," I growled.

"It's not a cat joke. It's a short joke, and it's not much of one since you are, by all accounts, short enough to blend into the scenery. That was why we hired you and your father, after all." She reached behind a dumpster, grabbed a holster with a laser pistol, and threw it around her chest. Then, she pulled off her brown wig, revealing a bright green mohawk underneath, and tossed on a black leather jacket, which she also kept behind the dumpster. "Now, if we're done with the tea party, we should go before they—"

"Halt!" Three soldiers in black armor appeared at the near end of the alley, holding laser cannons. "You are under arrest. Move, and we vaporize you."

"And that's what you get for asking so many questions." She turned to me.

"What do we do now?" I asked, my heart pounding as I looked for a way out. There were plenty of ways of egress for myself, but I wouldn't leave my savior in the dust. *Not yet, at least.*

"Don't worry. I'm full of surprises." As she raised her hands into the air, she tapped a black bracelet on her wrist. Before her hands were fully extended, two drones shot down from the rooftops and fired at the soldiers, who had no choice but to duck out of the way. With them momentarily distracted, Mouse grabbed me from the ground and cradled me in the crook of one of her arms.

"Let me go!" I screamed. "Don't you know cats eat mice?"

"I thought you weren't a cat, little one." She unsheathed the gun from its holster and fired it over her shoulder, knocking a hole in the brick wall that caused rubble to cascade down on the ground, blocking one of the soldiers from following us. "You're welcome to go it alone if you want. I don't think you'll get far without your nanites."

"How did you know I don't have nanites?" I asked as we reached the far end of the alley.

"Call it a hunch. I'm good at hunches."

As we exited the alley, a police hover car screeched to a stop in front of us while a squad of officers rushed our way from the far end of the alley. Mouse holstered her gun and tapped her wrist before the cops could raise their weapons, and leaped into the air, landing one foot on either of the drones as she buggered off through the air. I wasn't a fan of flying, even in a hover car, so being exposed to the elements held aloft by two drones caused me to panic as if I were a deer caught in headlights.

"Look out!" I managed to eke out as Mouse dipped below a taxicab that worked very hard to bisect us, dislocating our heads from our bodies.

Luckily, Mouse moved like the drones were a part of her, weaving deftly between the minuscule gaps between the cars that shot past us. They were, by and large, running on autopilot and trained not to take any life if they could help it, but I didn't want to test that theory. I had seen enough mishaps in my 17 years to know that not even a robot was infallible.

"I think we're losing them," Mouse shouted over the heavy wind that blasted us.

"Saying stuff like that is the kiss of death!"

No sooner did I say that when we turned a corner, and ten police hover cars, a swat team, and four armored trucks blocked our way forward. It wasn't thirty seconds before another wall of police cruisers blocked the way back.

"Well, this is more squad cars than I expected," Mouse said.

"That is an understatement," I replied.

"Relax. I know a thing or two about police cruisers." She smirked at me, and as she did, four of the cruisers crashed into each other in front of us, leaving a gap down the middle. "Namely that we've had a backend into their system for months."

We shot forward through the gap. They didn't fire, too nervous to hit their comrades, which allowed us to put distance between them and us before they could turn and catch up.

"Now," she said, "how about we find your father, huh?"

"Yes, please," I said, not realizing I hadn't heard from him since we left the facility. "Pop? Are you there?"

"They are probably jamming frequencies. You should be able to hear him in three, two, one..." As we passed under a big neon cowboy from a bygone age, Jammer's voice screeched into my ear.

"Skritch!" he shouted. "Can you hear me? I'm broadcasting on every frequency, cat, so if you can hear me—"

"I can hear you!" I screamed back.

"Where were you, Skritch?" he screamed. "I lost you on all scans. Where are you now?"

"Relax," I replied. "Somebody from The Spike found me. We're headed your way."

"You should get rid of that earpiece," Mouse said. "They can track just about anything."

"You're right," I replied. "Pop, I have to go. I'll see you in a little bit. We're headed your way."

Despite his protests, I pulled out the earpiece and tossed it on the ground as the wind whooshed by my hair and the police sirens grew dimmer in the distance.

CHAPTER 5

As we moved from the center of the Old City toward the outskirts, the lights dimmed until we were in nearly complete darkness by the time we entered the Bunghole. Mouse turned on the high beams on her drones for guidance. It had been close to an hour since we lost the police in the middle of the city, and while it was only twenty minutes as the crow flew to our hideout, we made serpentine motions to avoid detection and made sure nobody was following us. Once we were both sure our coast was clear, only then did I punch in the location of our secret base of operations onto the bracer on Mouse's wrist.

Jammer was incredibly cagy as to its location. Only six creatures in all of Zhakatal knew the base's location. We had a business fixing hover cars and basic handyman work, but that was only the legitimate front for the hacking business that kept us busy most of the time. Two of my cousins, Ballister and Node, ran the shop for us, and we funneled out illegal gains through it to keep up appearances.

We tried to work with upstanding organizations like The Spike, trying to bring down corruption inside major corporations, but I would be lying to say we weren't more mercenary than that. We took the work that came our way. Jammer was a talented hacker, and I was a gifted thief, but it was a big city without enough work to go around, so we all got by any way we knew how, which meant working for anyone who would have us.

"Over there," I said as we neared the ship graveyard that Jammer used as a base of operations. It was pretty disgusting, but the internet in the graveyard was the fastest in the whole city. We spent many nights planting tech all over the graveyard to create a powerful network, and the sheer vastness of the place allowed us to come and go as we pleased without worrying that we would be seen by prying eyes.

I pointed toward a large spaceship that had crashed over a hundred years ago. They gutted everything salvageable from the behemoth already, but what remained still made an effective amplifier that connected the routers across the graveyard while still giving us the privacy we needed.

Mouse set the drones down and tapped her wrist to power them off. I pushed through a slatted door turned on its side, and into the carcass of the ship. Some of the outside metal façade had been stripped for salvage, but much of it remained, nearly completely rusted through and useless. We worried that it would collapse on us if we sneezed the wrong way, but it was the only one like it in the whole junkyard.

I was careful not to touch the beams that bisected the path in front of us. We had placed traps all over the place in case we were invaded. Only Jammer and I knew the way through, and I carefully disabled the tripwires and pressure plates for Mouse as we continued forward, slowly and methodically.

It took several minutes to make our way through the hovel of the ship and make it to the bridge. When we did, I saw Jammer's console, complete with a dozen monitors and a glowing keyboard that had keys from a hundred languages and wrapped across the length of the table. It was his pride and joy. I often thought he loved it more than me, even when he assured me it wasn't true.

"Jammer!" I shouted, my voice echoing off the piles of metal and detritus scattered around the room.

"Get away from my son," Jammer's voice growled from behind us. I turned to see him holding a laser cannon at his hip, pointed directly at Mouse. "Now!"

"Whoa, whoa, whoa, Pop," I replied. "What are you doing? She saved my life."

Jammer stepped forward, his left leg wobbling under him. "Oh, Skritch, you talk a good game, but when it comes down to it, you really are gullible. She's not here to help us." He sneered at Mouse. "She's an assassin."

The muscles in Mouse's face held a look of fear for a moment, but then it eased into a sly smile. "You are good, old man. I'll give you that. No wonder they want to kill you."

"Who wants to kill me?" Jammer growled.

"Lots of people, actually," Mouse replied. "You have a habit of pissing off powerful people, it seems. Now, those debts have come to collect."

CHAPTER 6

"What are you talking about, Mouse?" I asked indignantly.

"I'm sorry, kiddo." Mouse grabbed me by the scruff of my neck and pulled me up with one arm while unsheathing her gun and cocking it with the other. "But maybe you are just a stupid cat."

I didn't have my nanites, and I didn't carry any other weapons, so all I had were my claws. I swiped at Mouse's face, but it was too far away, so I switched tactics. I dug my claws into her jacket, expecting her to wince and drop me, but she didn't do anything but laugh.

"Stupid kitty. Don't you think I would be prepared for that? This is platinum weaving. It can stop an anti-aircraft gun. I think it can handle your claws."

"I'll kill you!" Jammer said, shouting at her. "Let Skritch go!"

Mouse bopped her wrist with her nose, and a few seconds later, her two drones burst through into the fuselage, their guns spinning up to fire. Meanwhile, Mouse jammed the gun into my belly and snarled.

"Stop right there, or the kitty gets it."

"I'm not a cat!" I screamed, swiping at the air in the most indignant way imaginable, trying anything to break myself free. "And you are *so* going to die!"

She jammed the gun into my ribs hard enough that my body ached in pain. I was scrappy, but my bones were weaker than even a small human's strength. "I said shut up!"

"Wait!" Jammer shouted, holding up his hands. "Don't hurt her."

"Then you'll come with me willingly?" Mouse said with a smirk. "I expected more from the legendary hacker, but I guess I found your weak spot. I can't believe you would risk your life for a stupid cat."

"I'm not a cat!" I screamed, scratching at her with my back claws.

"Skritch!" Jammer shouted. "Stop! You're not helping!"

"I don't care!" I screamed, swiping wildly at the air. "I'm not going to hang here doing nothing while she hurts you."

"Sometimes, it's in doing nothing that we find everything, kiddo." Jammer walked up and pliantly placed his hands in front of him. "Let my daughter go, and I'll come with you."

Mouse looked at me and then Jammer before turning to one of the drones and placing me in one of their pincers. "Hold this one. Don't let her go until we're out of the hangar."

"That's not the deal—" Jammer said before Mouse smashed him over the head with the butt of her gun.

"I told you I would let her go, and I am. I just didn't tell you when. Did you really think I would give you a chance to get away before you were safely imprisoned?"

Jammer ground his teeth. "And how do I know you'll let her go when we're gone?"

"You don't, but you lost your advantage when you acquiesced to me. Don't you know anything about negotiating, Jammer?" She kicked him in the face, sending him backward. "Amazing you've been a thorn in our side for so long."

"And who is 'our' ?" I screamed as the drone carried me higher into the air. "Who do you work for? Gensys?"

She was completely focused, but in that moment, saying the word Gensys caused her to chuckle and turn to me. "My employers are smart enough not to conduct business out in the open, and I am smart enough to keep their secrets."

"You know what?" Jammer growled. "The deal is off!"

Jammer rushed forward and slammed into Mouse, sending her to the ground. He leaped on her, trying to pull the band off her wrist. It was at that moment I knew it was time to act. The drone held me tightly, but it couldn't feel, so I had the advantage. I flipped my legs onto the arms and used the leverage to pull my one hand free. Then, I reached up with my metal arm and used it to punch through the exoskeleton of the drone's wiring and pulled out every wire I could find.

"No!" Mouse shouted, but by that time, the drone was sputtering and shooting out black smoke as it teetered to the ground.

When it was five feet off the ground, I leaped off and rushed across the ground to help Jammer, who looked at me and shook his head.

"Get the other drone!" he shouted. "I think I can handle one little mouse."

I nodded and rushed to the other drone. I wasn't tall enough to swipe at the beast, but there was debris everywhere, and I knew it like the back of my hand. I had spent many afternoons practicing my agility with a long metal pole that had once reinforced the hull. Now, it lay dormant. I grabbed it from the place I left it and used it to vault off the ground, pushing off at the last minute to force-kick the drone, latching on at the last second when the drone spun out of control.

Drones were formattable in the best circumstances, but they were not great at independent thought or dealing with unexpected incidents, especially when those incidents included people trying to kill them.

The drone fired wildly into the air as I used my cybernetic arm to rip the guns from their carriage and turn it back on them. It only took two laser beams to the chassis before it started to spin out of control. I leaped off before it hit the ground and exploded.

"Enough!" Mouse shouted. I turned to see her holding my father, who hung limply next to her.

"I wanted to take your father in alive out of respect for his career, but the bounty says dead or alive, and you've forced my hand."

Mouse's face contorted into a twisted smile as she raised the gun to Jammer's temple and fired. The light went out of his eyes, and he fell to the ground in a lump of meat, dead.

CHAPTER 7

"*JAMMER!*" I screamed, rushing toward him. I didn't even care that Mouse had a gun, but as I moved toward him, she didn't fire. "*Pop!*"

I didn't cry often, but the tears were so thick in my eyes I could barely make out Jammer's body in front of me when I finally got to it. It was still warm, with the thick smell of burnt rubber coming from the wound in his temple.

"Pathetic," Mouse growled, stowing her gun back into her shoulder strap. "It's not even worth killing you."

The anger in her voice filled me and replaced the grief washing over me. My claws extended from my mechanical arm, and I lunged at her. I wasn't much of a hand-to-hand fighter without my nanites, but I didn't care. She wouldn't get away with killing my pop.

I swung back with my claw and swiped forward, but Mouse's boot met my chin before I connected and sent me flying backward, tumbling into a pile of loose debris.

"It's amazing you two could evade capture for so long, seeing as how inept you are."

I pushed off the debris cluttered over me and grabbed a pipe tightly in my hand. I rushed forward again. Mouse didn't move from her spot. She simply pulled out her gun and fired twice, once into the elbow joint in my cybernetic arm and another into my cybernetic knee, exploding both from the inside and tipping my balance over until I crashed into the ground at my dead father's feet.

"I'll kill you," I shouted as she neared me with her gun.

She drew her gun to my head. "I can see why they didn't put a hit out on you. Every piece of acclaim you got came from riding on your father's coattails from the moment you were born. It would be a mercy to kill you." She fired her laser gun into the ground next to me and holstered her gun. "That is enough reason to keep you alive, knowing this will eat at you for the rest of your life, and there's nothing you can do about it except agonize over how you could never beat me, not in a million years."

"I'll find you," I replied, growling. "I'll find you, and I'll destroy everything you love as you watch and weep."

"I look forward to it, cat." She turned and walked away. "I can tell you from experience that killing someone is an empowering feeling, but be careful; the thrill of having absolute power over another life is intoxicating."

I tried to push myself up but fell again to the ground. If either my arm or leg was taken out of commission, I could have stood a chance, but with her disabling both, I was as helpless as a newborn whelp. It was then that she decided to prove her point, pulling out her gun one last time and firing it in a concentric circle around me.

"But a word to the wise, if you come at me again, you better not miss. I won't be so generous next time. Now, I recommend you get out of here before the police come."

"You didn't—"

"Of course I alerted them!" she screamed. "Don't you understand that you're the bad guy here? I am the hero, no matter how you cut it. You are criminals, and I'm going to make a mint on your bounty on top of my normal fee. On top of that, I'll be called a hero. I like the sound of that."

"You're not the hero here. You can't murder somebody and call yourself a hero."

"Why not?" She replied with a sneer. "People do it all the time. Look at you, justifying your existence like you're the hero of your own story."

"I wasn't a hero. I was never a hero." My face fell, and I swallowed my pain. "Jammer was, though. He was always looking out for the little guy. He believed in truth, justice, and freedom. He wasn't a mindless killer."

She scoffed. "When you get a bit older, though—if you make it out of this alive, that is—then I hope you'll look up your pop and see what kind of stone-cold bastard he really was while you rot in jail."

"Jail?" I asked.

Her sneer turned into a smile. "Oh yeah. Didn't I tell you? That's the best part. You get a lifetime in jail to think about what you did.

That's assuming they don't kill you first, of course. How long do little kitties live?"

I screamed out at her, ripping every bit of my suffering out of my soul and throwing it at her, but that's all I could do, and she knew it.

"You're dead," I said. "Do you hear me? Dead!"

"No, sweetheart. That's your pop." Sirens howled in the distance. "Now, I have to go meet the police and collect my reward." She slipped into the frame of the fuselage. "I really do wish I could see you try to wriggle out of this one, though. I'm due for a laugh."

Then she was gone, leaving me alone with my grief. I tried to follow after her, but every step found me crashing back to the ground again. I howled out in pain as I pulled myself onto Jammer and curled up on his robust stomach. I pressed my head into the crook of his neck and wept into his lifeless corpse.

I must have nudged something loose as my sobs quaked his gelatinous belly because a few moments later, something crashed onto the ground. I looked up to find a circular recorder. Jammer often used it to record messages for clients they would discover later. He didn't love communicating with anyone over a live channel. He tolerated it with me during missions, but only because he managed every bit of the process...or I guess he did.

I uncurled myself from Jammer's stomach as the recorder rattled and fell open. From it, a ghost appeared, and then Jammer spoke, and seeing his holographic face caused me to weep.

CHAPTER 8

"Skritch, if you're listening to this, then the worst happened to me," the recording started, and I had already begun to bawl heavily. "Don't blame yourself for this. I know you will want to, but this isn't your fault."

He was trying to make me feel better, but it didn't matter what he said. I still brought a murderer into our hideout, and Jammer was dead because of it. "What I want more than anything is for you to find a simple life and settle down. I never should have dragged you into my life, and now that I am gone, I hope you can find the will to start over."

That's a nice thought, but he had to know I would never—

"However, I know you won't be able to move past this until you find the person responsible and enact justice. I want to be clear; I don't want that to happen, but I know you won't be able to help yourself."

Damn right, Pops.

"I recommend finding The Spike, and maybe they can help you."

Oh great, just find an organization more secretive than even we were. *Great idea.*

"This might be easier than you think. I've spent a lot of time trying to find our employers, and I keep my work stored in a secret compartment under the desk in my office in the garage. Only you can open it. When the time comes, you'll know how." The image began to fade away. "And Skritch, know that I love you, no matter what."

The video ended, and I grabbed the recorder with my only good hand. The police would be here any moment, and I didn't have much chance of escaping. Then, I noticed something in Jammer's hand: a black band, the same one Mouse used to control her drones. I pulled it from my father's hand and wrapped it around my wrist. One of the drones had exploded in a fiery crash, but the other hadn't blown up.

I peeked my head up and craned my neck to find the drone, and when I finally located one two piles of junk over, I crawled with my good arm and leg over to it. The sirens were right on top of me now, and I only had a matter of minutes.

I popped open the chassis of the drone and began to reconnect the wires that I disconnected, one by one, threading them between my toes to hold them steady while my hand moved like lightning between them. It wasn't comfortable work, but I was blessed with great dexterity, and before long, the spark came back to the drone's body. I popped the chassis tight again, and the drone buzzed to life right as a dozen officers rushed in and drew their weapons.

I didn't have time to test out the controls. I secured myself on the top of the drone and pressed my hand on the strap. It whirled to life and lifted off the ground. Two of the officers fired at me as I rose into the air. I looked down at the band and noticed that it pulled down a set of controls, including one that showed two guns firing.

I pressed that button and the turrets on the front of the drone spun toward the officers and began to fire on them, causing them to duck. I only had a moment, but it was enough to find my bearings and tilt the drone up toward the ceiling.

As we rose higher, the laser fire started again, and I banked into the rivets and piping of the fuselage, weaving in and out for protection as the cops fired on me.

"There!" I shouted at nobody but myself when I found one of the many holes in the fuselage that we had patched over the years.

I pushed the button for the drone to fire at the weak spot, and it easily burst through the paneling we had used to patch it up. The sky was alight with red and blue lights. We burst through the fuselage and banked hard right to avoid two police cruisers stationed in the sky as they fired on us.

I maneuvered enough so they didn't hit me, but one of the laser blasts hit the droid, and it immediately sank. I did a lot of damage to it earlier, and it had nothing left to recover from a laser blast from a police cannon.

I tried to pull the droid up from its nosedive, but when I knew it was impossible, I waited until it was just above the ground and tucked a roll onto the dusty ground below. The fall didn't kill me, but I felt a rib crack as I tumbled along the ground, and another one snapped when I crashed into a broken ship.

Every breath was agony as I tried to push myself to stand, but my balance was all off, and I couldn't do more than slip back to the ground. As the officers rushed toward me, screaming for me to get on the ground, my eyes lost all focus, and I fell into unconsciousness.

An inauspicious start to my revenge, to be sure.

CHAPTER 9

I woke up to the jostling of a car. Hover cars generally had pretty good hydraulics and gyroscopics to keep them level in the air, but in traffic, they tilted from one side to the other as the force of other cars moved past them.

"She's up," a bearded orc officer said from the passenger side front seat. "We thought maybe you died."

I pushed myself up with my one good arm to find I was strapped tightly in the seat. "Is that why you bound me so tight?"

"Well, in fairness, you were alive when we threw you back there," a broad-chested mutant officer said from the driver's seat. "Besides, better safe than sorry, right? We know how skilled you are at evading capture, and you're such a tiny thing that if you somehow got away from us, we'd probably never find you again."

"Except that there's not very many cats with a cybernetic arm and leg in Zhakatal. Kind of makes you stand out in a crowd."

"I'm not a cat," I growled at them. "I'm a crypto—"

"We don't care," the broad-chested one interrupted. "Or, more accurately, it doesn't matter to us."

"But it matters to me. I'm still a citizen of this great city, so maybe you should give a crap about what I want."

"You're a criminal," the first officer said. "Your needs don't matter."

"I still have rights, and unless the law has changed, I'm innocent until proven guilty by a court of law."

The broad-chested one cackled. "See, saying stuff like that shows a complete lack of understanding about how the justice system actually works."

I knew it was true, but it was off-putting to hear them say it so blatantly. Most officers at least acted like the rules mattered to them, even if they were just doing it as lip service. Having them abandon the ruse meant they must have been deeply corrupt.

"How long have you been on the take?" I asked.

"Now, that's not information we're just going to offer up, cat," the first officer said. "But let's just say that your chances of getting out of this alive are very minimal."

"So you say." I looked up to see that the red light that usually blinked to show that a car was being recorded was off. "My lawyer is going to know something is up when they can't find the recording of this ride."

"We know," the broad-chested one said. "But without a recording, there is deniability."

"That's going to be suspicious, don't you think?"

"Nope. Half the cars in this fleet are so old they're being held together with little more than duct tape and hope."

These officers were deeply corrupt, and they had no fear of being found out, which meant whoever they reported to was just as corrupt and used to covering their tracks. Heck, their whole department might already be corrupt, and the rot likely didn't start there. Corrupt officers became corrupt detectives, who became corrupt supervisors, who became corrupt chiefs, who became corrupt commissioners. The police department had been corrupt since before I was born.

That wasn't to say every officer was rotten to the core, but it was rarer and rarer with every passing year to find one who wasn't on the take. Sometimes, that worked out in our favor, though, because that meant they could be bought.

"How much are they paying you to keep me out of the system? I'll double it."

They both laughed before the broad-chested one caught my eye in the rear-view mirror. "I don't think you can afford it, kitten. Especially not since we seized all your accounts with the arrest."

"What?" I shouted. "You can't do that!"

"You'd be surprised what we can do. It's evidence, baby," the first officer said. "It's not our fault if we skim a little off the top before it gets turned over to the bosses. So, I guess, in a way, you have already paid us."

The blood boiled in my chest. "I'll get you back for this. I swear it."

"With what?" The broad-chested one scoffed. "We have everything. Your computers. Your hideout. Your chop shop—"

My cousins. "Stay *out* of our garage. You won't find anything there."

"Well, that's not true," the first one said. "I'm sure you've funneled illegal money through that shop, which makes it an illegal front, and we will go through every inch of it. When we find evidence of money laundering, we'll arrest anyone working there, too."

"And if we can't find evidence, we'll make it up."

"Exactly."

My heart jumped into my throat. If that was true, it was only a matter of time before they found the information Jammer left for me. It was too late to save Jammer's life, but I would be a monkey's uncle if I would let them take my cousins away from me...or my vengeance.

But I had to be careful with what I said. Anything I said would incriminate me, and if I upset the officers, they would make my life a living nightmare and make escape impossible. No, I needed them to lay their guard down, like Mouse did. If they thought I was helpless, they would loosen their grip on me, and I would be able to find their weakness.

"I have to admit," I said, "I've been nabbed by officers before, but they've always been easy to elude. You seem to have yourselves together, and for the first time in my life, I'm legitimately nervous I might spend time in jail."

"You should be," the broad-chested one said. "We have the best arrest record in the whole department."

"That's impressive, officers," I replied in my least threatening voice. "How do you do it?"

"Good instincts, of course, and dogged determination," the first one replied.

"And it helps when you're not above planting evidence," the broad-chested one chuckled. "But you have to be smart about it. How you plant evidence, when you rough up a perp, and how you elicit a confession…it's all a dance."

"It's true," the first one added. "It's really more an art than a science, like painting."

"And you paint with the blood of criminals, it seems," I said.

"Hey!" the broad-chested one said. "I like that. I'm gonna steal it."

I shrugged. "Go for it. You've already made it abundantly clear there's nothing I can do about you stealing from me."

"You got that right," the first one laughed. "Almost a shame we have to take you in. You're the pliable type, and I like that about you. You would make a good informant, assuming we could keep you in line."

"Toeing the line is my specialty. It's kept me alive more than once," I replied in a whisper.

"Well, keep it up," the broad-chested one said. "And you might survive this, too."

"Highly doubt it, though," the first one muttered as I turned to the window. "But a positive attitude never killed anyone."

No, I thought, *Mouse did that, but you won't. I will have my revenge.*

CHAPTER 10

"You look fine," a doctor said as they examined me in the infirmary of the police station. "A few bumps and bruises."

Any time a perp was apprehended after suffering injuries, it was customary to take them to a doctor, but they didn't say it had to be a good one or one that wasn't on the take as well. This doctor was neither good nor clean.

"I think my ribs are broken," I replied. "Every breath is agony."

"Nonsense," the broad-chested officer said. "And now that that's done, I believe we have a beautiful cell for you."

Their smile was off-putting as I opened my mouth to speak. "There's nobody around but us and this doctor you're paying off. I don't think you need to sell it so hard. I know what I'm in for. I've heard enough stories."

"But you haven't seen one of our holding cells." The other officer had a gold tooth and crooked smile that I didn't notice until they stood in front of me. They were hideously ugly, with a gnarled, bulbous nose that seemed to have been broken no less than a dozen times. "This is going to be a treat, then."

"For us, at least." Their partner wasn't just broad-chested; they were broad everywhere, down to their ankles and wrists that pulsated against a uniform that seemed destined to burst at the seams any second. "Come on, then."

The utter humiliation of being tossed into a cat carrier for transport through the station was not lost on me. It was the most degrading experience of my life to watch officers of every species, size, and creed point and make jokes at my expense as I was led through the station. It seemed they made a point to parade me into every corner of the department so each officer could take their shot before we finally descended into the basement into the harsh, dank holding cells that seemed out of another century.

The broad-chested officer touched her hand against a metal pad next to the furthest cell from the door, and the metal grating slid open for her. The bulbous-nosed officer opened my cage and tossed me onto a hard bed.

"Don't get any funny ideas." The broad-chested one typed into the pad, and the bars slammed down again; the spacing between them was too small for even me to fit through. "We have cages for all sorts around here, even wee things like you."

"What's going to happen to me now?" I asked.

The bulbous-nosed one shrugged. "That's not our department. We'll see you at the trial if you make it that long. I wouldn't hold your breath for that, though."

"I would practice holding your breath, though," the broad-chested one said. "They like to waterboard around here."

"Don't you know that torture is a terrible way to get the truth?"

"Maybe," the bulbous-nosed officer said. "But it's a great way to get a confession."

They high-fived and then walked away, leaving me to rot. Luckily, even though my body was broken, my mind was alive the whole time, mapping out the entirety of the police station, from the entrance to the captain's office to the holding cells. I estimated it would take me thirty-seven seconds, sprinting at full speed, to make it out of the station and into one of the hover cars parked outside. They would be on me immediately, so I would have to make it down to ground level quickly, where I could get lost in the shadows of the building. We weren't far from the Bunghole, and if I could get back there, I could disappear and recuperate.

Of course, that left me with a conundrum because I only had two limbs working right now. Both my cybernetic arm and leg were busted. If I had my nanites, I could create new limbs for myself, but without them I was a sitting duck, unable to create a new limb from scratch. Jammer's tech was a combination of organic and inorganic materials. Even a crude replica would require a machine shop to cut new limbs for me, but maybe I could find a way to rig a crude crutch that would at least service me until I could find something better.

I hopped down from the bed, my lungs burning like fire, and hobbled over to the cage. Not only was the filament too small for me to squeeze through, but even the gaps shimmered with the tell-tale signs of a forcefield.

I instinctively touched my ear for my comm, only to realize too late that I had taken it out when I was with Mouse. Even if I still had it, there was nobody on the other line. Jammer was dead. With me in jail, I wouldn't even be able to bury him properly. He didn't believe in the afterlife and even refused to discuss uploading a backup of his consciousness to the cloud for the future. He was a stubborn mule like that, and it broke my heart that I would never be able to hear his stupid, gravelly voice again.

I never thought I would miss his barbs so deeply as I did, but it ripped at my heart more than the broken ribs I surely had, and I collapsed on the floor in a heap. I tried not to cry, but it was no use. The emotions overtook me, and every heave of my body was agony, but it was a good pain. It reminded me I was still alive, at least for now.

CHAPTER 11

They kept me in that holding cell for what felt like a week, slowly turning down the temperature more and more until it was so cold that I could see my breath. When I was sure that the frostbite was about to come for my other arm, a doughy police officer finally pressed his mitt against the pad next to my cell, and the bars slid open.

"Cold enough for you?" they said with a smile.

I was confident I would come up with a plan during my confinement, but even after all the time I had to think, I had no way of escaping. I thought of bolting through the officer's legs, but even if they didn't catch me, somebody else would. I simply wasn't lithe enough to escape, not with both an arm and a leg missing.

"Funny," I replied with a snarl.

They stepped away from the cell for a second, and I thought I had an opening, but a moment later, they pulled a cat carrier from just out of my view and placed it in front of them. "Get in."

I would not suffer that indignity. "Make me."

Their eyes narrowed, and the smile washed from their face. "If you don't get inside, I've been instructed to neuter you."

"You don't neuter female cats, idiot."

"Then you admit you're a cat, then?" The smile came back on their face. "Now we're getting somewhere. You have five seconds, or I'll get the spray bottle. My cat hates the spray bottle."

I wasn't a cat, but I hated the spray bottle all the same. Who wouldn't? Being sprayed with water is demeaning and unsophisticated. "Fine."

I ambled forward slowly into the carrier. I didn't want the officer to touch me, and I knew that was the only way forward if I didn't cooperate. I needed to cooperate until an opportunity presented itself, after all, and I hoped I would find a way to escape before I ended up dead.

The carrier was easier than being picked up by the scruff of my neck, but the officer swayed me like I was on one of those pirate ships at an old-timey carnival, and by the time they slammed me down on a metal table in an interrogation room, I was nauseous enough to vomit all over everything.

When I stumbled out of the carrier and looked at the officer, they smiled again. "If you vomit, we'll charge you with vandalism. So, keep it to yourself."

The officer knew exactly what they were doing, and I even heard them chuckle on their way out of the room, proud of themselves, probably on their way to stuff their face with a donut. The thought of it made me want to wretch, but I believed the officer that vomiting would not be looked upon kindly, so instead, I lay down on the table and tried to calm myself by breathing.

I knew the game. Somebody who was flustered, emotional, and angry was less in control of their mouth, so they were more likely to spout out something that would incriminate them.

Criminals were generally antisocial loners who often had problems controlling their emotions. Gangs recruited those who fell through the cracks, those who lived in bad homes or didn't have homes at all. Criminals were often easy to manipulate emotionally unless they were trained well. Even then, needling perps usually got a reaction over time.

Picking scabs caused you to bleed, after all, even if a wound was healing well. Criminals often wore their wounds on their sleeves. Most of the time, those wounds were what brought them to crime in the first place, and many never let their wounds heal at all, exposing themselves like a raw nerve to the world.

I knew I was loved, but watching Jammer die, the person I loved most in the world, snuffed out by some unknown force, deadened that part of me. Being captured by a corrupt institution that worked for those same murderers, well, it was my raw nerve, and they knew it. I didn't know what they wanted me to say, but I knew this: I would not let my emotions get the best of me. That wouldn't get me any closer to finding out who killed my father, and—

My pep talk to myself was cut short as a lanky detective in an ill-fitting suit stepped into the room. "Good morning, Miss Skritch. It is Miss, correct?"

"No need to be polite. I know you plan on killing me." I kept my eyes closed. "Why are you keeping me here?"

"Well, that's not an answer, but I'm going to assume it's a yes." The detective pulled out a metal chair and sat down at the edge of the table. "I'm Detective Martinez. My pronouns are she/her."

"I knew you were a detective from the smell of your cheap perfume and poorly fitting suit. You're trying to look the part of respectability without the money to pull it off." Two people could play the game of pushing each other's buttons.

"I can feel the hostility in your voice."

I opened my eyes. "My father was just murdered in front of me, and you all have been calling me a cat since you put me in here, insulting me, laughing at me, and trying to get under my skin. Wouldn't you have a little hostility in your voice if somebody misgendered you or called you—" I noticed the pointy ears poking through her hair. "A human, even though you're an orc."

"I'm an elf," she said, clearly hostile. "But point taken."

I sat up. "I have nothing against cats. I'm just not one, but to answer your first question, yes, it is Miss, but most people call me Skritch. I don't talk to many fancy people like you're trying to be, *Miss* Martinez."

She nodded. "Good, maybe we can get some real work then. Why don't you tell me what happened in your own words?"

I chuckled. "So I can implicate myself? I don't think so. Why don't you tell me what you know, and I'll let you know if you're on the right track?"

"You were found in proximity to a dead body, Miss Skritch. I want to help you, but—"

"If you met with the bounty hunter like she said, then you know I wasn't the one who murdered my father. Now, if you want my help, it's best not to lie. You want to help yourself, Miss Martinez, and what will help you is getting a confession. You're not going to get one of those because I am not guilty. I'm also not an idiot." I leaned back in the chair. "Don't I get a phone call? I'd like to call my lawyer."

"You don't want to do that, cat. It will get very complicated if you do."

I smirked, an idea suddenly forming in my brain. "Well, at least I know your courtesy doesn't go very far. I think I'll make that call now, though. I know you've already made up your mind about me, but I would at least appreciate the ability to play the role of innocence, even if you've already made up your mind about me."

She stood. "I should have them sic a dog on you, cat, but as you wish. If you want to drag

somebody else into this with you, I'd love to
know how deep your criminal enterprise goes."

CHAPTER 12

It was a dangerous card to play, as there was just about as good a chance that they would arrest my lawyer than let him talk to me, but I had to risk it. We didn't so much have a family lawyer than a community one; a thick, stocky ogre with warts all over his face who made it his life's work to speak up for criminals in the Bunghole.

We paid him handsomely for the privilege, but he absolutely loved the law in a way I would never understand. There were things that I loved as much as he loved law — but thieving and sneaking were objectively way cooler and more interesting than boring law books.

The detective and I stared at each other in silence after I made my phone call. It was the one thing guaranteed to piss off a cop, not answering their questions because you were smarter than the average criminal they interrogated.

"Your attorney is not going to save you," she said, folding her arms in front of her.

"No, I don't suppose he will, but it is pissing you off something fierce, and that is its own reward, truth be told." I had taken a seat on the edge of the table where I could see the silhouettes behind the door. "I suppose you'll put words in my mouth no matter what I say in the end."

"That's how it works," she said, pointing up to a surveillance camera. "That's just for show, and we can fake your paw prints easily enough. If that all goes to pot, we could just kill you."

I leaned forward. "Oh, I wish you would. You do know where I live, right? Killing me would be doing me a huge favor."

"We would prefer you kill yourself," she said, deadpan.

"I'm sure you would, but I won't give you the satisfaction of doing your job for you—" I narrowed my eyes at her. "At least not until I get revenge on Mouse and everyone who set me up."

"Is that a threat?" she asked. "Should I add that to the list of charges?"

I shrugged. "Do what you want; that's what you're best at."

"That's not true. We're good at protecting the people who run this city from the likes of you."

"That's to be seen, love." I smirked at her. "We're like cockroaches. Stomp one of us, and three more will rise to take my place."

There was a knock on the door. The detective stood up and opened the door. A being with a radiant face of shocking blue leaned forward and mumbled something to her. The sneer on her face brought great joy to the cockles of my heart and told me that my attorney, Doug, had arrived.

She didn't speak to me as the lumbering ogre pushed through the door that was barely able to fit him. People made fun of Doug when he went off to school, but when he came back with a degree and started getting us off on all sorts of charges, we grew to respect him as we should have all along.

"Thank you for keeping my client company, detective," Doug said, not turning back to her. Instead, he placed a briefcase on the table and flipped it open. From it, he pulled a jammer and flicked it open. "I'm sure you can understand that we will need privacy."

"Using those is illegal. I could have you arrested."

Doug turned back to her, sizing her up for the first time. "If you could arrest me, detective, then you would have years ago. So let us not pretend here." He pulled out another device and turned it on. A cone formed around the two of us, and when the detective started to talk, it was like she was a hundred yards away. "She'll get the hint soon."

"Are you trying to piss her off?" I asked as the detective flung her hands in the air and stormed out. "Cuz I think it's working."

"Of course I am. Nothing grinds my gears more than traitors. She used to be on our team, you know, but somebody came along with a better offer, and she flipped."

"Yeah?" I said. "And whose team is she on now?"

Doug shrugged his huge, muscular shoulders. "I don't know. If you could find out, that would be lovely."

"You are very, very confident for a lawyer whose client was found dead to rights."

"Yes, but you aren't dead," Doug said. "Which I consider a win, so we have something to work with. Now, how are you doing?"

"I'm okay." I looked down at my busted arm and leg. Sadness tried to crash over me, but I refused to give in to the pain. There would be time for grieving later after I sliced Mouse's neck from ear to ear. "Just need a repair shop."

"I'll let you lie to me, just this once," Doug said. "But if I'm going to help you, then you need to be honest with me."

I nodded. "Fair enough."

"Now, tell me everything."

"That will take a while," I replied.

"Then it's a good thing I cleared my schedule."

CHAPTER 13

Doug sat silently as I finished my story. He took out a tablet and wrote notes by hand with a stylus, but aside from the occasional grunt or "hrm", he simply let me speak without interruption.

When I was done, he placed his pen on the tablet and smiled, but it didn't last long before it fell into a frown. "I would like to be honest with you, if you would let me, about your prospects."

I nodded. "That's why we have you on retainer. I don't need a friend; I need a lawyer."

"Good, I agree." He placed his meaty paws on the table and took a deep breath. "In that case, I can say you are absolutely screwed. There is absolutely no way you will make it to trial, and even if by some miracle you do, then they will not allow you to leave a free woman."

"Don't you think I know that?" I leaned forward. "You don't need a law degree to see that, Doug. What am I going to do about it?"

He cleared his throat. "Your cybernetics…I assume by their condition that you don't have access to your nanites, then?"

I shook my head. "If I had them, we wouldn't be in this position. I would have slit Mouse's throat by now."

He held up his hands. "I am a lawyer. I can't hear that kind of thing."

"I'm sorry," I said, dropping my head. "I didn't lose, though. I'm still alive, and that was her first mistake."

"Well, you are stuck in here, so..."

"And that's where you come in...yes?"

Doug rubbed his forehead. "I am not a criminal, Skritch. It is the one thing that has kept me out of prison. I work with alleged criminals, yes, but I am not one myself. I must maintain an air of respectability."

"Then," I growled, "I'm screwed."

"I'm sorry," Doug said. "I am happy to be a friend in this time of—"

"I don't need a friend!" I shouted. "I need somebody with thick skin who can help me get out of here."

"And that is not me."

"Maybe you can talk to one of your clients and—"

"NO!" Doug's voice boomed. "Don't put this on me. I have a family to worry about."

"And mine was just taken away from me."

"I know." Doug dropped his head. "There is one possibility. How much money do you have, liquid, right now?"

I chuckled. "Crime pays well, but you know that the lifestyle is expensive. All the money we have is tied up in that garage, which I'm going to assume has been seized by the police."

"That would be my assumption, too, so there is no collateral to negotiate your bond."

"This is depressing." I looked up into his big, green eyes. "Do you think you could get a message to my cousins? Let them know I love them."

Doug smiled then and reached into his bag. "Actually, I have received a letter from them. Kind of antiquated, but they said you would appreciate it."

"I never was one for technology, even though I'm made of it, so this is fine by me."

Doug pulled out a square envelope sealed with red wax. "This has already passed inspection, and they have allowed me to give it to you. However, I was told that you cannot open it until you are back in your cell, alone. Those are your cousins' wishes."

Wishes or instructions? I didn't know what they were planning, but my cousins loved technology. Part of the way we bonded was when they would fix my cybernetic circuitry. I had a habit of causing it to malfunction, especially in my youth, and Jammer was often too fed up with my antics to deal with me when I destroyed his beautiful work.

"Thank you."

"You don't have to thank me. This is my job."

"It's not just that. You are a good friend, and...I really could use one of those right now."

"I thought you didn't need a friend."

"Yeah, well...I'm also an idiot."

I reached forward and placed my paw on his huge, wart-filled hand. The instant I did, a red light filled the room. Even though I couldn't hear it through the tech Doug had, I knew an annoying voice blared "no touching" in a high-pitched squeal.

With that, a red-haired police officer rushed inside and slammed a carrier on the table. "I think we've had just enough of this. In you go."

Doug stood. "Do you know how demeaning this is for her? She is a Cryptophage, not a cat, and deserves to be treated with respect."

The officer shrugged. "Don't care much. Just carrying out orders."

"Yes..." Doug growled. "But I see in your eyes the glee you take in demeaning my client."

The officer smiled. "So, what are you gonna do about it?"

Doug knew better than to say anything incriminating. He'd spent his life navigating the murky gray area of the legal system, and even before that, it wasn't like he had been treated well in his youth. Ogres were always considered to be bad news, and more than once, I heard somebody say that evil ran in his blood, which was a shame because Doug was the nicest, most understanding being I had met in my time because he knew what it was like to be treated differently.

"It's okay, Doug," I said, slipping inside the carrier. "There are battles to be fought, but we have to pick them, right?"

Doug nodded. "Indeed, Skritch. Until we meet again, and we will meet again."

"I believe you, Doug."

CHAPTER 14

I didn't know what my cousins sent me, but they hated ancient technology like letters. If they had something to say, they could have included it in an email, recorded a voice message, or even posted a video. Instead, they chose to write a letter, the most inconvenient and low-tech way they could have communicated with me.

No, there had to be something else inside the letter, whether Doug knew about it or not. Regardless of whether he did or didn't, Doug would be investigated if something in the letter helped me escape. I only hoped they cleared it with him first because it would be hard to keep him a free ogre if something nefarious happened to the client that he was representing.

I could barely hide my excitement when the police officer brought me back to my cell and locked me inside. They didn't bother frisking me or confiscating the letter I held tight in my hands. If they could have kept me from reading it or thought it was dangerous, they would have already stopped it—the fact they didn't meant everything.

I used my broken arm to crack the seal of the letter and pulled it from the envelope. Dust plumed from the letter and made me cough loudly. Oh, if only that were nanites, I would be free in a matter of minutes, but there was no way to sneak something like that in for me.

I tilted my eyes down at the letter and examined the chicken scratch handwriting that was certainly my cousin Ballister, the older and more seasoned of the lot, and who generally spoke for the two of them.

Skritch,

This is a right fine mess you've gotten yourself into. The police have taken the garage, and they won't even let us see our uncle to say goodbye. I always knew you would be the death of him and tried for my whole life to separate the two of you. He had the faith in you I never did, and now I can say it was misplaced. If he hadn't taken you in all those years ago, he would be alive, and I can't help blaming you for that.

The police have tried locating us and have yet failed, but we have instructed Doug to negotiate on our behalf to spare our lives in exchange for testifying against you. If he should be successful, I suppose we will see each other on the other side.

If you happen to get out, please don't look for us. You are dead to us now, and you were never part of my family.

*I hope you rot in there for what you
did to my family.*

-Ballister

By the time I was done, I could barely breathe. My chest was tight, and the tears came, thick and wet. I heaved as I wept big, sloppy tears, lying prostrate on the ground. The letter fell from my hand and drifted across the room until it came to rest next to the bars, but I did not care to save it.

They were my last hope for salvation. They were my last family left, and now, I had nothing. As an orphan, my greatest fear was being abandoned. Over the past decade, though, Jammer made me feel like I had a home and a family. My cousins accepted me, or at least I thought they did. I built a life, and now it was all striped away from me.

Stupid Skritch. You were right to worry all along.

Now, the reason they let the letter through made sense. They wanted to destroy the last of my fight and force me to confess. There was nothing to protect now. There was no reason to live. There was only—

—And then I saw something from the corner of my eyes that pulled me from my pity. The light from the forcefield sparked for a flickering second, and a blue light emanated from the paper. I thought it was a trick of the eye, but then it flashed again, and I knew it was not an illusion.

I picked myself off the floor and dragged myself over to the letter. My stomach was tight as I slid forward one awful step at a time. The forcefield hadn't flickered before. In fact, I barely knew there was one unless I looked for the telling shimmer when you glared at the shield from a certain angle that warped and distorted the reality behind it.

But now, it sparked and fired every few seconds like a downed power line. I picked up the letter and held it to the light, which sparked more violently the closer I held the letter to it. In the glow of the light, I smiled, looking down at the block letters of my cousin Node, written in a blue pen.

> *Sike. We knew they would let that pass. We love you, Noodle. Throw this paper into the forcefield and stand back.*
>
> *Love, Node*
>
> *P.S. - Don't forget to cover your eyes.*

I couldn't contain a smirk as I slid backward and crumpled up the paper. The flickering of the shield stopped as I moved backward. I didn't know what they had planned, but they were family, and I trusted them.

I wound up and chucked the paper toward the shield. As it neared, the light started to crackle again, and when the paper hit the forcefield, it exploded into a million little particles that rained down. As they touched my skin, they started to blink and flicker before running down my arm and leg. As the rain touched the bed, the flickering particles began to disassemble the metal bunk and ground it into a malleable powder.

Nanites.

When they were done pulling metal from the bed, they met with the nanites on my limbs and began repairing the work that Mouse destroyed.

CHAPTER 15

It was definitely janky, but after a bit of work, the nanites my cousins smuggled into the holding cells for me reconstructed a crude but effective set of replacement limbs that worked well enough for me to walk normally. They were heavier than Jammer's craftsmanship and listed slightly to the left, but beggars couldn't be choosers, and I was definitely the former.

Unfortunately for me, the nanites were not built to last. Of course, they couldn't be because the scanners would pick up on those, but if they were created flimsy enough to disintegrate after one job, then they could be constructed to avoid the scanners.

These were something of Ballister's own construction, meant to dissolve once their work was done. I had never seen anything like them before and looked forward to picking my cousin's brain about how they made the technology behind the nanites, but first things first. I had to get out of the jail, which meant outmaneuvering at least thirty officers, as I made my way up the stairs, through the bullpen, out the front door, and down the fifty-story drop to the ground below.

I was a special type of thief, but I wasn't magic, which meant I needed to find a set of keys on my way through the station that would power a hovercar I could use to finish my escape.

It was a lot, and I would likely fail, but I had one thing on the police: they didn't suspect anything. They thought I was a stupid little cat, and I would make them pay for that in every imaginable way.

It wasn't long after I finished that an officer came to give me dinner. This wasn't one I had seen before, but they had a pronounced jaw and bushy eyebrows. It was night now, which meant the night crew was on. Hopefully, that meant an understaffed police station, which would make my exit easier.

"No funny business," the troll growled with a thick accent I couldn't place.

I had wrapped myself up in my blanket to hide my new limbs and readied myself to pounce. "Please, I'm just a useless, broken cat, right? What do you have to fear from me?"

The troll sneered at me and placed his hand on the pad to open my cage. When the bars receded, they walked inside and placed down a metal bowl filled with kibble, the last insult they would ever give me.

I waited until the troll was off-balance before unfurling my blanket and leaping off the bed. They didn't even have time to react before I smashed them in the jaw with my cybernetic arm. It was heavier than Jammer made it, and that heft was rather helpful in punching through fools. My ribs burned in pain as I landed back on the ground with a groan, but the troll was down.

To think, if they had just estimated instead of underestimated me, they would have come down the stairs with a team of guards instead of one. Their hubris got the best of them.

I rushed out of the bar and passed another holding cell with a grizzled tiger cryptophage inside of it. "Hey! You're free. Get me out of here!"

"Sorry, buddy. I don't have much time."

"Do you really think you can escape on your own?" they growled. "You need me."

I could handle myself, but maybe they were right. A hulking cryptophage would do a lot of damage upstairs. I leaped onto the wall and dug my hands in as I smashed through the pad with my cybernetic arm. It really was coming in handy. It didn't take much to overwrite the wiring and free the tiger. It was child's play.

"Don't make me regret this," I said to the cryptophage when the bars came down.

"Oh, I won't. I will carve a path of destruction the likes of which you've never seen."

I smirked, and then I looked back to the other cells. All manner of criminals were hidden behind bars, and a thought occurred to me. If two bruisers were good, then a half dozen were better.

"Pick him up," I said, pointing to the troll.

Using the tiger's strength, we were easily able to use the troll's handprint to open every holding cell and release a half dozen criminals back into the world, and all of them had a chip on their shoulder.

"Let's burn this place to the ground!" I screamed.

The criminals roared with excitement and rushed forward toward the stairs. Before I went with them, I patted down the officer and found a set of keys to their cruiser. *Those will do nicely.*

I hadn't even gotten up to the bullpen before I heard the chaos of overturned desks and gunfire coming from upstairs.

I walked gingerly, with the pain in my ribs growing with each step, but eventually, I made it up the stairs. When I entered the station's bullpen, it was chaos. Dozens of officers worked to quell the rebellion, but they were focused primarily on the big monsters that could take out a half dozen of them at once. They didn't even pay attention to a little cat that held to the shadows. They made fun of me for my size, but if I were any bigger, I would have drawn the officers' notice.

Instead, I was able to slide through the station, avoiding blaster fire and fistfights before I reached the front of the building. I looked down to find "24" written on a chain around the keys.

The officers usually tasked with guarding the cruisers had long abandoned their posts to go inside, which allowed me to snake through the parked cars until I found one labeled 24. I turned the keys and gunned it into the night. Once I was far enough away that they couldn't chase me, I let myself take a big breath, and a smile crested on my face.

It's about time something went my way today. Now, it was the simple matter of revenge.

CHAPTER 16

I crashed the hovercar as quickly as I could, safely bringing it down to the floor of the city. They would track it soon enough, and I couldn't take the chance they would follow me before I could get lost. I had a much better chance of disappearing in the underbelly of the city, anyway. The police weren't much concerned about what happened in the lower areas of it.

We could kill each other for all they cared, as long as we didn't impede on respectable society, and that was exactly what The Spike was all about, showing that society was rotten, and taking down the capitalist pigs that used money to avoid wallowing in the mud with us.

If anyone could understand my plight, it was them, but finding them was nearly impossible. Jammer knew how to do it, but his secrets were locked inside our old garage, which had been seized by the police already. I was in no shape to take on the whole of the police department in my current state. I needed to get bandaged up and get a game plan before I stood a chance of exacting my revenge.

My leg and arm grew heavier with each step. The beauty of Jammer's design was that it combined high durability with easy maneuverability. The steel of my cot wasn't nearly as lightweight, and I didn't have the physical strength to carry it far. By the time I got half a mile from the hovercar, my thigh and shoulder ached along with my ribs, and every time a police cruiser flew overhead, the sound of their lights prickled my spine and turned my stomach.

I needed to get off the street quickly, and I only knew of one person that I trusted in this area of the city. Pop trusted him to fix him up when he'd been through it, which was good enough for me. The only problem was that he was a veterinarian, which dug a dagger into my pride, but my father told me that if you were ever in real trouble, you called a vet. They had to work with hundreds of different species, and most of them couldn't talk back, which meant there wasn't anyone for them to spill your secrets to, and loose lips sink ships, as the saying went.

Doctor Svorkin was a dwarf, which made me bond with them more than most. Even if others wanted to slight them, nobody would ever dare raise a slight to an enormous bear that could slice them through with razor-sharp claws.

I hobbled into their clinic after the open sign had been turned off, but the door was still open, and the bell over it worked just fine to announce my entrance. There was nobody at the front desk, and it took a long moment for the doctor to step through the comically small door.

"I'm sorry." They adjusted their glasses. "But we're closed."

"I know." I dragged myself toward the counter. "I need your help, Doc."

"I specialize in pets, my child, not cryptophages. I think you've been mistaken—"

"I'm not mistaken. You helped my pop, Jammer, out of a few jams over the years, and while he's not around anymore, I still need your help."

"Jammer…" They choked back their sadness. "What do you mean he's not—wait, he's dead?"

I nodded. "That's right. He was murdered almost ten hours ago by an assassin named Mouse. I aim to find her, but I can't do it looking like this, feeling like this. Can you look me over, Doc, for old times?"

The doctor narrowed their eyes. "For as many times as your father helped me, it's the least I can do. Lock the door and turn off the lights. Then, come in the back, and I'll take a look at you."

I did what the doctor asked and joined them in an exam room. By the time I got there, the shutters had been closed to prevent light from seeping out to the outside.

"You're a pro at this," I said with a smirk.

They patted the exam table for me to sit down. "Your father was not the first, nor the hundredth, criminal I've helped over the years. I dare say they are my best customers and take the best care of their pets, might I add."

"You a criminal, too, Doc?"

They shook their head. "Nothing like that. I just have a fondness for broken things."

The doctor examined me, rotating the sore joints of my cybernetics and examining the craftsmanship of my cousins' work. They listened to my chest and forced me to take painful breaths. After half an hour or so, the exam was over, and they looked at me with kind, though pensive, eyes.

"What's wrong, Doc? Am I going to die?"

"Well, strictly speaking, we will all die before long. It just depends on the time horizon you look at. In the life of a cockroach, we are ancient. In the eyes of a star, we are specks of time, but eventually, even they die, and it will be nothing but blackness for trillions of years."

"That is bleak, Doc, and a bit too philosophical for me. So, I guess I'm narrowing the focus. Am I gonna die in the next, say, day or so?"

"I can't say that either, especially if your aim is revenge. I can say that none of the injuries you have right now will kill you. I'll give you an injection, which should heal you right up and leave you feeling right as rain. Of course, it won't help your cybernetics."

"That's okay, Doc," I said. "I think I know how to fix those if you're willing to make a call for me."

"As long as you don't tell me what illegal things I'm being culpable in, I think I can do that. I need some deniability, after all."

"Don't worry, Doc. I'll keep you out of it as best I can. I just have to see a lawyer about some nanites, if you catch my drift."

"Not even a little bit, and I thank the heavens for that."

CHAPTER 17

I needed sleep, and it would take time for Doug to arrive, so while the doctor made the call, I took a short rest. I don't know how much I slept, but I woke up to banging on the door. Doug's gruff voice echoed through the room. "Open up! I am not a courier, and I will not stand here for more than one minute before leaving."

Doctor Svorkin walked to the front door and, after confirming the voice through a quick tech check and finding no manipulation of either the voice or the body, opened the door and let Doug inside.

"I'm sorry—" I started before Doug held up his hand.

"Do you have any idea the level of trouble you're in?"

I nodded. "I have some idea."

"Oh good, well, at least you're not a complete moron. Do you know how much trouble I'm in for this little stunt? I'm going to have to go into hiding for this one."

"They were going to kill me, Doug. You can't possibly expect me to stay silent and let them kill me while Jammer's murderer is out there."

Doug sighed. "No, I suppose not. I wish you had let me handle it, but I was frank with you that your chances were bleak at best and tragic at worst, so I suppose I can't blame you much."

"I am not a patient woman," I replied. "It's one of my biggest weaknesses. I saw an opening, and I took it."

Doug's eyes narrowed. "I suppose your cousins smuggled something in with that letter I gave to you?" He bit his lip. "No, don't tell me. I need some level of deniability if they find me."

"Can I suggest we take this in the back?" Doctor Svorkin asked. "Where we have sound dampening and better lighting manipulation."

We agreed, and Doctor Svorkin led us through the office into a small room in the back, which looked more like a bomb shelter than anything you would find in a vet's office. There were hundreds of cans and supplies, but also knives and guns interspersed throughout the cabinetry.

"Are you going to war?" I asked Doctor Svorkin when they closed the door behind us.

"You never know in this city," they said. "You could be living your life, minding your own business, and a wanted felon enters your establishment with their lawyer. You have to be prepared for anything."

"A being after my own heart," Doug said. "Now, as I was saying, every officer in the city is chasing you after what you've done. There is a million-credit bounty on your head. They do not like being shown up."

"I suppose they captured the inmates whom I helped escape?"

"They didn't catch everyone. The tiger cryptophage you helped is also on the loose. You have no idea their rap sheet, Skritch. You helped free one of the biggest crime lords in the city."

"I thought they looked familiar." I thought back and placed them as the head of the Zchar crime family. Their name was Vazia, and they were famous for hijacking police tech and selling it to criminals to keep themselves hidden. Jammer and I had several of their toys in our hideout. Of course, it doesn't help keep you hidden if you lead the bad guys right to your base. "And they're charging me with their escape?"

"Among other things, and I've been alleged as a collaborator to your plan."

"That's crazy," I replied.

"It doesn't matter," Doctor Svorkin said. "Since when have the cops not jumped to any convenient conclusion that suits their needs."

"Exactly," Doug replied. "I've gotten my family into hiding for the duration, but the only way to clear my name is to lead you to them and plead my freedom."

My face dropped. "Please tell me you didn't."

"No, I haven't yet, for old time's sake, but I need to give the cops something to pave this over in 24 hours, or it's my head on the chopping block."

I couldn't let them take Doug. He wouldn't do well in prison. He was too used to the finer things in life. Besides, I very much liked his wife and child. I didn't want them on the run for the rest of their lives.

"I will fix this," I replied.

"The only way that will happen is if you bring yourself in."

I chuckled. "Yeah, I don't see that happening, but I swear to you, Doug, I will clear your name. You have my word on that."

Doug cocked his left eye to me. "If it were anyone else, I would turn you in myself, but your word is your bond, so I will trust you. Please, don't let me down."

"I won't," I replied. "But in return, I need you to take me to my cousins. They need to upgrade my tech if I'm going to figure this whole thing out, and now I have a ticking clock over my head on top of everything else."

"I would normally warn you against bringing your family into this, but since they were responsible for bringing mine into this scheme of yours, I'll be all too happy to bring you to them. If anything, you can all go down together."

"We're not going down, Doug." I stepped forward. "I swear to all that is holy, by this time tomorrow, you will be eating dinner with your family in your house, and these charges against you will be a thing of the past."

"You had better be right," Doug said, turning to Doctor Svorkin. "And for your help, I'll make sure you are well compensated, either through Skritch's estate or by the bounty on her head. Can I count on your discretion?"

"A million bucks is a lot of money," Doctor Svorkin replied. "But I have way too many clients who would see my loose lips as a liability and take me out before I could spend any of it, so I will keep your secret."

"Thank you," Doug said. "I will make sure my other clients know of your discretion."

"Well," I clapped my hands together. "What are we waiting for? Time is ticking. Let's rock and roll."

CHAPTER 18

"I'm going to ask you to trust me," Doug said as we walked out of the vet's office. "Even when every bone in your body tells you not to trust me, I need you to keep the faith. Can you do that for me?"

"Absolutely not," I said. "That sounds like the type of thing somebody who was definitely going to turn you in would say."

"I know you have a problem with trust." Doug chuckled dismissively as he shook his head. "But if I wanted to turn you in, I would have shown up with a half dozen police cruisers."

I couldn't deny his logic, but that didn't make me like it any less. Something felt off, but if I was going to put my faith in something, anything, then there were worse places to lay it than at Doug's feet.

"I can't say I'm not gonna lash out at you, but I'll try to tamp it down and keep my trust in you for as long as I can."

Doug opened the back seat for me. "That's something, I suppose. We'll work on the rest. I thought that getting your father off on those charges a couple of years ago would have earned me more faith than that."

"Oh, it did. Every bone in my body's telling me to run right now, so just the fact we're having this conversation shows a level of trust I heretofore didn't know I possessed."

I hopped up into the back seat, and he closed the door behind me. When he entered the car as well, the car turned on with a mighty roar, and the windows fogged up with a dark tint that made it impossible to see inside from the outside.

"This is not my first time transporting a wanted felon, but it is the first time I've been one as well."

"I'm not a felon, and neither are you. They only call you a felon once you're convicted. Until then, we're both alleged felons. I thought your fancy law school taught you better than that."

I expected the car would divert further toward the Bunghole, but instead, it spun toward the middle of the city and took off with a lurch. Doug's hands were clenched tightly on the steering column, even though it was clear the autopilot had kicked in once we rose into the air.

"What are you so nervous about?" I asked.

"Literally everything," was Doug's reply. "I work with a lot of criminals, but my life, outside of a few terse moments, is pretty boring. My child, whom I love more than life itself, only knew what I did in passing and from the errant newspaper headline that we passed during our morning constitutionals. They are not used to this kind of scrutiny. I am not used to this kind of scrutiny."

"Have I apologized for that yet?" I said. "If not, then I am really sorry about all of this. When you're in the thick of it, you lose the forest for the trees and just put one foot in front of the other. I didn't think about who I hurt along the way, but it wasn't my intention. I just want to do right by my father."

Doug nodded from the front seat. "It's all we can ask of our children, to do right by us, but you might be surprised by what we consider 'do right by us'. To me, it's not about revenge or justice. It's about living a good life and doing better than we did. All we can hope is that we've given you the tools you need to survive."

"That sounds like real sweet thinking, but my pop wasn't a sweet man. He wanted revenge, as sure as my name is Skritch. He told me himself in a recording he made just before he died."

"I have no insight into that, but I talked to Jammer a time or two in my life, and he didn't seem much different than me in what he wanted for you. In fact, he lamented more than once that he dragged you into this life. I think it was just above his capacity to provide for you both in any other way."

"Yeah, well, we don't all have fancy law degrees, and I'd be willing to wager if some assassin came to kill you and your kin, you would have a much different take on the matter."

Doug thought for a second. "I can't say you're wrong because I've never been in that position, but I have talked to my share of criminals in my day, and enough of them were dads that I think I can confidently say, if you gave up and went away, then you would be a lot happier in the future."

"Maybe that's true, Doug," I replied. "But I can't see those trees yet. Right now, I'm in the forest, just trying not to get lost."

"If you scratch this itch, you might not like what you find."

"That's the smartest thing you've said yet. I'm sure I won't like what I will find, but I can't stop now, buddy."

"No, I don't suppose you can, and I'm really sorry to hear that."

It was then that all the doors locked, and a partition went up between Doug and me. I tried to remember what Doug made me promise, to trust him even when I didn't think it was possible. When four long, black hover cars pulled up around us, it was hard to keep the faith.

CHAPTER 19

"What's going on here, Doug?" I asked, breathless, as I scratched at the windows.

"Remember what I told you?" Doug said. "Your cousins...they have taken up refuge with a gang you know very well... The Gigahertz."

The name sent shivers down my spine. Jammer and I worked for the Gigahertz a couple of times back when I was getting my feet wet in the crime game. This was back when they were a band of no-good toughs and thugs and needed some tech wizards to help them move up in the world. We thought they would be better for the city than the then-reigning overlords of The Bunghole, who were called the Zha.

Quickly, we realized we were wrong. While the Zha were ruthless and cutthroat, they had a soft spot for the mean streets and took it easy on us whenever they could. When we helped the Gigahertz take down the Zha, we replaced benevolent criminals with sociopaths. Gone were the days of being late on payments, and gone were the days of saving innocents from the fray.

In a lifetime filled with mistakes, helping them rise to power was the worst by a factor of about a million.

"That's impossible," I replied. "Ballister would never do that in—"

"They didn't have a choice," Doug said. "The police came down hard on you guys. Add on that a million-credit bounty on your heads, and...well...let's just say there weren't a lot of places that would offer safe harbor. The Gigahertz took pity on them. They're always looking for good tech help, and your cousins are two of the best mechanics in the city, now that..."

He trailed off, but I knew what he was going to say. "Now that Jammer is dead, you mean?"

Doug nodded. "It all happened fast, and if I didn't help them, well, then you would all be arrested, and there would be no hope for you. I know how much you hate Gilles, but they are about the best chance you have at the moment."

I growled at him for a long moment. "You asked me to trust you, and this is what your trust brings? You should have just brought me to the police. I would have a better chance of survival there."

"I can open these doors and let you drop to your death if you think that's a better situation. Otherwise, I suggest you listen to what Gilles has to say. It might just save your life."

I slid back into the seat. "I'm not helping them."

"Even if it means getting your revenge?"

I didn't say another word, but the truth was that I would do just about anything to find Mouse and whoever put the hit out on my father. There had to be powerful factors at play if they involved the police. They were corrupt, but they weren't cheap, and getting the whole of the department to focus on us meant that whoever pulled the puppet strings was very well connected.

"Just do what you have to do."

Doug nodded and rolled down his window. Another car pulled up alongside him and opened theirs as well.

"Is that her?" a gruff voice from the other car said.

"My client is in the back and ready to speak with Gilles."

"Open the door, and we'll come for her."

Doug shook his head. "I told you before, I'm going with her to the meet. I've already cleared it with Gilles, and if you don't like it, I suggest you take it up with them."

Doug's voice was forthright and forceful but not rude. He was used to living in this world, walking the fine line between criminal and victim. It showed with every move on his deliberate face. He made no sudden moves but also didn't look away when the person in the other car spoke.

"You are lucky you are worth more than the trouble you are causing."

"If you do not want my client's services, I can always go down the list. She might be the city's most wanted criminal right now, but you know her worth as much as I do."

There was a groan from the other car. "Follow me."

Doug nodded and put up his window. "See, that wasn't so bad."

"What part of 'I'm not working for them' don't you understand?"

"Well, here's the sticky wicket of it, Skritch. We're dealing with a house of cards here because the only way I was able to get your cousins' protection was by promising to get you out of jail. I didn't know if I could do that or not, but I figured it would buy them some time. If you died in jail, I had backup plans, but here you are, alive and well, for all intents and purposes. Gilles likes me, and you, but they aren't known for their kindness, as you well know. So, I suggest you at least hear them out, and if you don't like what they have to say, then we can make other arrangements, but as your lawyer, I highly suggest you like what they have to say."

"You're putting me in an impossible situation, Doug."

"No," he replied as the four black hover cars encircled him. "Whoever hired Mouse and ordered the death of your father did that. I am just trying to keep you alive with the raw deal you were dealt."

"You're right." I dropped my head. "This isn't on you. Thank you for helping me, even if it's in ways I absolutely hate."

He put the car in gear and followed the procession. "Yes, that sentiment is shared by most of my clients. Fortunately, many of them are alive today because of me. I'd like you to be one of them."

"I don't much care if I'm alive...as long as Mouse is dead."

CHAPTER 20

Our procession weaved through the city until it finally descended into the 20th story of a building that seemed like it had been built back when twenty stories was an impressive feat. We had long past eclipsed that point. Now, even 200 stories seemed quaint.

When we were docked, two gang members dressed in black suits, their signature look, stepped out of each car. I didn't know why one would join an illegal operation that had a dress code. The best thing about being a criminal was that nobody told you what to do or what to wear. Of course, if the price was right, I would do just about anything, and the scum that worked for Gilles would do more for less than me.

"Do not speak, and don't look anyone in the eye until we're in front of Gilles. I can't tell you how bad it would be for both of us if you did."

"Relax," I replied. "You act like you don't trust me, and trust goes both ways."

Doug sighed. "I know how you get when you're stressed. You like to flap your lips. Whenever you get that impulse, squash it."

He stepped out of the car and submitted to a pat down from the guards in front of him, even though it seemed like he could throw them over his shoulder and still have enough energy for a hike—*the things we do for our family.*

I closed my eyes and took a deep breath. I swore to myself I would never come to see Gilles, no matter how bad things got. I swore on Jammer's life. Maybe it was fitting that I came here now after my father was dead.

"Lift your hands!" one of the soldiers said when I stepped out of the car.

I fought every impulse to deck them and did what they told me. A mutant knelt and patted me down. Most of the crew was made up of mutants and orcs, the kind polite society didn't much like, and even fewer tolerated. That was the appeal of Gilles. They gave purpose to the disenfranchised and taught them how to be powerful in a world that sought to strip them of it.

"She's clean," the mutant said. "No nanites, and these cybernetics aren't much good on a twerp like her."

I wanted to sock the mutant in the jaw, but that would violate my pact with Doug something fierce. Plus, they were right. Even after getting help from the vet, I could barely lift my arm, and my leg felt heavier with every passing step. I feared my hip would pop out of its joint any second from the struggle to lift it. I almost...ALMOST...longed for a carrier, but I would never be treated like that again. I would die first.

Our procession pushed Doug forward and led us down a series of corridors with doors, behind which I suspected were all manner of accountants and lawyers doing what they could to keep as much of Gilles's money off the books as possible. On the floors below us were warehouses filled with illegal guns, drugs, tech, and a data center where the best techs in the galaxy worked all manner of jobs to build Gilles's wealth ever greater.

"Doug!" we finally heard as the hallway broke into a large club made up mostly of bars and a dance floor. A purple-skinned dragonoid stepped forward, and I knew it was Gilles. When they came to Zhakatal, they originally brought nothing with them and were able to use their forked tongue, both literally and figuratively, to amass enough wealth to protect themselves and build an army that would rival the Zhakatalan Planetary Guard.

Still, their organization was mostly built in The Bunghole, and despite all their power in our neck of the woods, they had yet to crack in anywhere respectable businesses cared about, and that gave them quite a large chip on their shoulder.

"Thank you for having us," Doug said.

"It's so wonderful to see you," Gilles kissed Doug on both cheeks and smiled. "I'm so sorry to hear what is happening to your family and hope to get this nasty business behind us now that you have brought me a friend."

"That would be lovely. They are safe now, thanks to you."

"Please, after all you have done to keep my people out of jail, this is the least I could do to repay you." Gilles turned to me. "And here, we have Skritch. You are a tough cookie to track down. It took monitoring a dozen police scanners to find you, and not a minute too soon, either."

I looked over at Doug. "Is this the part where I speak?"

Doug nodded. "If they're asking you a direct question, yes."

I turned to Gilles. "I hate you and everything you stand for. If you hurt one hair on my cousins' heads, I will jam my cybernetic arm so far down your throat it will come out the other end."

Gilles looked at me hard for a second and then laughed. "Oh, my. Not many speak to me the way you do, Skritch. I would think that a threat if you weren't such a puny little thing. Still, you need not worry. Ballister and Node are two of my best mechanics. I wouldn't dream of hurting them. Of course...accidents happen. We work in a nasty business, you and I."

"We don't work in the same solar system, Gilles. Don't lump me in with you."

"Whatever allows you to sleep at night, but we are both criminals, and we both have a vested interest in taking down Gensys."

"I don't care about them. That's The Spike's problem. All I want is to figure out who set my father up and kill them."

"Then, that is something we can help with. It seems like we have a basis to do business after all."

"Oh yeah, and how can you help me?"

"Easily. I can get you into your cousins' garage to pick up the hard drive your father left for you, and all you have to do is one little thing for me."

"How did you—"

Gilles held up the recorder that the police must have confiscated from me. "I may not have the money to buy the whole department, but a well-placed bribe can get a lot of information if you know where to look. Now, you want to break into your old garage, and I need something your father kept inside it."

"And what is that?"

"The reason we didn't kill you as soon as you showed up, of course."

CHAPTER 21

"That is ominous," I said, deadpan.

"It's supposed to be." They cleared their throat. "But if you do this for me, I promise you will lead a long life...or at least, a life free of the threat I pose to your life."

"I guess that sounds okay, then. I have to get into that garage anyway, and this makes it easier," I replied to Gilles. "But just for my own edification, what exactly are you talking about?"

Gilles sucked their teeth. "Your father worked for me a lot longer than you realize. He was one of the first people I grew to trust on this backwater planet, and when nobody would give me the time of day, he offered to help."

I looked up at Gilles. "I don't believe you. He always told me you were the absolute worst."

They shrugged. "I don't really care if you believe me, and neither does the truth. For years, he vowed never to bring you into the work we did together, but one fateful night, we had no choice but to call on you." Gilles turned and started walking toward a door to the left of the room. "He never forgave me for bringing you into this life, but I think you ended up well enough in the end."

"He's dead, and I'm on the run from the law," I replied. "I wouldn't say that I'm doing well at all, truth be told, but please continue."

"Oh, we all have tragic backstories, kitten." Gilles smiled. "And that's not an insult to you as a cryptophage. It's just my little affectation. I hope you will grant me this one without anger."

"There are so many things that make me angry. I don't think insulting me, whether it's because of my race or my gender, even makes the cut, but still. Don't do it again."

"You're no fun, but fine. Now, where was I?" Gilles thought for a moment and then snapped their fingers. "Ah yes, your father's past and the nature of your mission. You see, I thought you were a superior operative and could be one of my best if I brought you under contract, but your father didn't see it that way. He thought I was a corrupting influence on you, and before long, even though I paid handsomely, on time, and with a smile, he grew a conscience and wanted to take you out of this life."

"Let me guess, you didn't take that very well."

"It made me angrier that he fell back into his old ways almost immediately." Gilles snickered. "But no, I didn't like it one bit. I wouldn't have made it far if I let my best people leave without consequences, so yes, I threatened. I was young and impetuous, but I stand by the fact that you would have done better with me than on your own. After all, did The Spike protect you from assassins? No. But I could have. I am, in fact, this minute."

My hands balled up into fists. "Did you send Mouse after us? Are you responsible for this?"

To this, Gilles cackled. "I'm sorry, my dear, but that's so humorous. If I wanted to kill either of you, trust me, I would have done it myself and taken great pleasure in it. However, I couldn't do that because your father created a failsafe against me that would trigger in case of his untimely death."

"Of course, he did, which is why you let us go without making a scene. I always wondered."

"Bingo," Gilles said, turning toward me. "And now, through no fault of my own, your father is dead, and the failsafe has been triggered. Only his kin can disarm it and prevent a very unnecessary kerfuffle in my ranks, which is where you come in."

"And how is that?"

"In your father's garage, there is a secret compartment, and the only being in the universe who can open it is you, with a biometric scan to prove you are alive. We worked for years to ascertain its location and ferret out the horrible fate that has followed me all these years, and now, in a fortuitous coincidence, you have walked into my domicile, able to free me from my long-suffering torment."

My eyes narrowed. "And what's to prevent you from killing me once you get it?"

"My dear, the failsafe has been triggered. In twelve hours, the dirt he has on me will flood the internet, so what is to stop me from killing you now if you choose not to help me?"

"Fair," I replied. "Then I suppose it's mutually assured destruction."

"Or mutually assured cooperation if we work together." Gilles held out their hand. "If you help me, then you have my word that no harm will come to you or your cousins. I would extend that to others you care about, but you don't have any of those, do you?"

"You have me by the whiskers, don't you?"

"It would seem that way, but I, too, stand on a precipitous ledge."

"Tell me, what does my father have on you?"

"I will not answer that, except to say it was a youthful mistake that would surely lead to my demise, no matter how much money I threw to make it go away." Gilles stepped backward, and their hand hovered over the latch on a door. "Now, will you help me, or will this get unpleasant?"

I stepped forward. "And if we help, you swear that my family will be safe. Ballister, Node, even Doug and everyone else I know?"

"I can't guarantee I won't come down on them for something they do in the future, but if you help me, we will wipe everything clean and start from scratch as friends. Trust me, you could use a friend like me right now."

"A murderous thug?" I said. "Yes, I can see that. Fine. I will help you. Now, where are my cousins?"

Gilles smirked and pulled the latch on the door. "Right here."

CHAPTER 22

"NOODLE!" Ballister shouted as I walked through the door. Gilles slid out of the way as two lumbering dwarves with short, trimmed beards stomped through the room as if they weren't imprisoned there. They weren't much for crime, so they might not have even known how much trouble they were in. "It's so good to see you!"

Node was considerably smaller than Ballister, but he was faster, too, which meant he got to me first and swung me around like we were in a cheesy movie. "You got heavy, buddy."

"You are just weak!" Ballister shouted, scooping me into his thick arms.

"It's good to see you both as well, but can you please stop swinging me around before I vomit on you? K, thanks!"

Ballister came to a stop and let me back down on the floor, where I stumbled through the room a bit before my arm finally came to rest on the wall behind us.

"Why do they call you Noodle?" Gilles asked from the doorway.

"You don't know that story?" Node said. "When Dad brought Skritch here home, we thought she was a stray cat for a minute, and seeing as she couldn't talk or anything, we called her Noodle for a whole year before she learned enough words to correct us."

"That is fascinating," Gilles said. "It's no wonder you hate being called a cat. Well, on that cheery note, I will leave you to it."

"Wait," I said to Gilles. "Doug. You are going to take care of him, right?"

Gilles noted. "He'll be fed and treated like a king. I guarantee it. It's funny that you worry about him because all he worried about, aside from his family, was you."

"We go back a long way."

Gilles nodded and stepped out of the room, closing the door behind them, which sealed with a loud sound, like all the air being sucked out of the room, and then we were alone, the three of us.

"How are you doing, sport?" Ballister asked.

"Terrible," I replied. There was no reason to lie to them. "Jammer is dead, and I'm being chased by the whole police force at the behest of some shadowy organization that wants my head."

"I know it's tough, kiddo," Node said. Even though they both acted like children, they were both in their fifties and well-established as expert mechanics. "We barely got out of that situation with our lives, and only thanks to Gilles."

"I wouldn't thank him yet. You're prisoners here, in case you haven't noticed."

"Oh, we noticed." Ballister stepped forward. "We're thick-headed, but not entirely daft, cousin. I know you don't think much of us, but you would have to be a complete idiot not to recognize a prison when we see it."

"I don't think you're *complete* idiots…just half of one, each," I said with a smirk.

Node chuckled. "Well, I thought only a complete idiot would destroy good tech, so why don't you hop up on our work table, and we'll see just how much you screwed the pooch."

I did what they asked and climbed up onto a metal table in the center of the room. For a prison, they had a ton of amazing tech to play with, all at the behest of Gilles, of course. As they said, it would be stupid not to use two of the brightest mechanics in the Bunghole when they came to you for help.

"Originally, we didn't believe he was dead," Ballister said as he looked over my arm while Node checked out my leg. "When Doug came for us, I nearly punched him in the throat at the implication."

"And I nearly kneed him in the crotch," Node added. "But Doug isn't one for jokes. He's a straight shooter. Probably why they sent him to us."

"So, Gilles sent him? Doug made it seem like he came of his own accord."

Ballister shrugged. "Maybe he did. It's kind of hard to nail down a timeline. All we knew was he got us out of there before the police came, just by the hair of our chins, which are, admittedly, long."

I looked over at Node. "Did they try to make you open anything while you were there?"

Node scratched his beard. "How'd you know? Yeah, they pulled back a carpet to reveal a little safe built into the ground we didn't know was there. Both of us tried to open it, but nothing happened."

"I suspected as much," I replied. "Seems that's what they want me to do, fellas."

Ballister narrowed his eyes. "But cops are probably still crawling over that place, combing it for clues. It's like you're begging to be caught."

"And after we helped you escape," Node grumbled. "Don't you have any gratitude?"

"Of course I do," I replied. "But we're in it now, boys. Jam—Pop's gone, and Gilles has us all trapped in here. I don't know about you, but I don't like cages of any kind, no matter how nice they are. If I don't get into that vault in the next twelve hours, then who knows what will happen."

Ballister and Node looked at each other and sighed. "Then I guess we better get your gear fixed so you don't get yourself caught."

I looked over at Node. "Don't suppose you have any nanites left, do you?"

Node nodded. "You know, we weren't behind you having them at first. But you're one of us in every way that matters, so we'll set you up with some before you go. Otherwise, you're a sitting duck."

"Just don't go losing them again, alright?" Ballister said. "It's not like they grow on trees."

"I promise," I replied. "And thank you."

"Don't thank us yet," Node said. "We're getting you prepped for a suicide mission. Save the thanks for when our repairs are good enough to get you back here safely, alright?"

"Alright," I replied. "I can do that. Meanwhile, I'm going to take a nap."

"A cat nap?" Ballister chuckled.

I curled up in a ball. "I will murder you later."

CHAPTER 23

It took longer than I imagined it would to unfuse the steel from my limbs and then reforge them with platinum, but by the time Ballister and Node were done, I finally felt like myself again for the first time in a long time...

...or, it wasn't really a long time, was it? It felt like eons had passed, but it was barely a day since my whole life was turned upside down. It was a little unnerving, thinking about how fast everything could go up in smoke and your life could be completely different than you ever imagined it.

"Give it a spin," Node said, clasping my arm into the socket for a final time. "It should be perfectly balanced now."

I hopped off the table and dashed across the room. "It feels good, really good."

Ballister smiled. "Better than Jammer's design, I'd wager. I've been wanting to try it out for a long time, but he was so protective of you he'd never let me mess with your limbs except to give minor alterations."

"This is a complete redesign using cutting-edge tech," Node added. "It should be lighter and stronger than even the steel you were wearing before."

I slashed at the air with my new cybernetic arm and then did a backward kickflip, landing perfectly on my feet and turning back toward them. "It feels great. I can feel the extra bounce in my step."

"Be careful with it." Ballister crossed his arms. "I'm serious."

"I am a lover, not a fighter."

"Please, you are the *fightingest* creature I've ever met. I watched you take down a mutant twenty times your size once."

"Alright, fine. So, I'm not opposed to a fight, but that guy was asking for it, and they were alone. I'm not about to fight the whole of the police force." I looked up at Node. "You can trust me on that. It's run first, ask questions later."

"I usually trust you, but I think you're lying to yourself. Still, I can't stop you." Ballister looked at me silently for a long moment. "This is still a daft plan, but at least you have the tech to pull it off now."

"What about the nanites?" I asked. "How do I sync with them?"

Node leaned down and pressed a button on my arm. From it, a cloud of nanites rose into the air. "You remember the incantation, right?"

It had been a long time since I had to bond with nanites, but I remembered the spell that connected them to me for as long as I lived, or they did. The nanites followed as I walked forward and let them surround my head like a swarm of gnats. I breathed in and let the nanites flow through my nose and out my mouth once, twice, and a third time. Then, I whispered the chant my father taught to me that every parent taught to children of our clan for as long as they had developed the tech to manipulate nanites.

Once the words were said, the nanites hovered silently for a moment. I feared I had done something wrong, but then, one by one, the nanites lit a blue light on their backs until my head was surrounded by hundreds, thousands of little lights, like fireflies in the darkness.

"You know," Ballister said. "The first time you successfully merged with nanites, it nearly made me cry. This time...well, heck, I need a tissue."

I took one more breath, and now the nanites were no longer inert. Now, they ebbed and flowed with me and my body. I was overcome with emotion, but there was no denying that the little devils were a handful to have floating around. When I blew out another breath, I commanded the nanites back to their place in my arm until they were needed.

As my vision cleared, I saw Node, eyes watery and lip quivering. This was a sacred ritual passed from parent to child, and none of us had any of those anymore. Jammer had looked after Ballister and Node since his brother and his brother's wife were killed on a transport mission twenty years ago. He never married, but he had three children all the same, and now we were all, truly, orphans. It never felt that way while Jammer was alive, except in the dark night of our souls, but now, there was no doubt.

The emotion overtook me, and I cried until there was nothing left, and then my back continued to heave as the weight of my sorrow cut deeply into my soul. Ballister joined us before long, and we knelt there in a big, blubbering pile of mess until the door opened once again.

"Oh, isn't this a pitiful sight," Gilles said. "Should I assume you are done then? Since that would be the only way there could possibly be time for blubbering."

Ballister and Node let me go, and I wiped the snot from my face. "We're done."

"Good, because we only have a couple of hours left, and it's going to take at least that long to get that device and prevent my horrible mistake from being plastered all over the internet. Luckily, we have not been idling. Everything is set for you as long as you're ready?"

"I'm ready." I looked back at Ballister and Node, then over to Gilles. "Let's get this over with."

"That's the spirit."

CHAPTER 24

"What is the plan then?" I asked Gilles, following them through the serpentine hallways of their pace. "I assume it's more complex than me simply breaking into the garage and hoping for the best, or at least I'm really hoping that it is."

Gilles nodded. "We've assembled the best team we could pull from other jobs. We have many other projects in the works, but this one is of the utmost importance, so I diverted our resources to this endeavor."

Gilles turned a corner into a large hangar where three rough-looking types were milling around a sleek, red hover car. It was the type of car they take waiting lists for, and only the richest of the rich could afford. I heard stories about the Frazetta 320's legendary speed and turning ability. It must have cost at least a million credits.

"Nice car," I said.

"Thank you. It's my pride and joy, so don't go ruining it, okay? There are only three mechanics in the whole city who have access to the parts and skills necessary to repair my baby."

"You realize you just about guaranteed we're doing to destroy it, right?" I replied. "That kind of talk is the kiss of death."

Gilles turned. "Let me be clear. If you destroy my car, I will place the kiss of death on you and your cousins."

"Fair enough," I replied, pointing to the crew around the car. "So, who are these jabronies?"

"Bull," Gilles pointed to a large mutant monstrosity at least twice the size of the rest of us combined, "is the muscle. They'll cause a distraction to pull guards off the door. I've already called in what remained of my favors in the department to lighten the detail on the garage, but even with all I've done, there is considerable protection around it. They seem to believe you will hit it soon and that capturing you there would be the easiest and best last chance to find you."

"They're smart," I replied. "I miss the days when the police were stupid."

"Yes, those were glorious times." Gilles pointed to a lithe goblin covered in leather and tech. "That's Xree. She's your tech help. Once you enter the premises, she'll shut down all tracers and video for two minutes."

"Hurry, though," Xree added. "Cuz usually the cops are quick to react when I mess with their toys."

"I'll be quick like a bunny," I replied. "I know exactly where I have to go."

"Don't you mean cat?" a grumpy-looking human with a garishly bedazzled jacket whose face looked like it had been melted in acid said. "Or are you the PC police?"

"This is John," Gilles said grumpily. "He's a lot to take, but he's also the best driver in the city. He's your wheel man, and if things go south, he'll get you to safety...or die trying."

"Shouldn't he be the one that gets the 'kiss of death' if your baby gets destroyed, then?"

"He knows the stakes," Gilles glared menacingly at the human. "Don't you, John?"

"Like my life can get any more miserable," John replied. "Can we get this over with, please?"

"Right," Gilles said, turning to me. "The plan is simple. The police have mostly finished investigating your garage. The only thing they can't open is the safe, but they have called in a techno mage to handle that, too. We have this moment to act. Luckily, most of the cops have been pulled off protection duty to another matter close by."

"What are they chasing?"

Gilles replied, "I gave them a hot tip that you have been spotted elsewhere in the Bunghole, and they are going to investigate. That leaves just a skeleton crew guarding the building and the CSI crew inside searching for clues. We can't do anything with them. You are just going to have to evade or attack them."

"I'll try one, and if that doesn't work, then the other."

Gilles nodded. "Whatever it takes, but remember you only have two minutes because the second you step into the place, Xree is going to jam everything they have, so don't dawdle. In the game of speed versus stealth, always choose speed."

"Maybe I can get you another 30 seconds on a good day," Xree said, "but it usually goes the other way, which means you're probably gonna have less than 2 minutes."

"Which is why we have John," Gilles said. "We assume you'll trip their sensors before you get out, so once you're clear with the package, John will be there to guide you to safety."

"Can you finally tell me what I'm looking for?" I asked.

Gilles shook their head. "I'm not quite sure. All I know is it will be a device that had a connection to your father's vitals, and the minute he died, a countdown began. We have ways to disarm it if you bring it back here, but remember, we're on a tight timeline."

"Then what are we waiting around for? Let's get this show on the road."

"A cat after my own heart," John said. "I'm dying of boredom here."

John stood, but before he righted his balance, I leaped on his chest and sent him tumbling backward. I grabbed his jugular with my cybernetic arm, choking him.

"I am not a cat. I'm a dwarf through and through, and my name is Skritch." I let go of his throat. "If I hear anything disrespectful coming out of your mouth ever again, I will literally make you eat your words, understand?"

John choked. "I get it! I get it! Now get off me!"

I backflipped off his chest and landed on the ground to a round of applause from Xree. "You are a creature after my own heart. His bad attitude is very grating. Don't worry about me, though. I know a cryptophage when I see it, and if you're on Gilles's crew, then you must be incredible at your job."

"I'm the best," I replied. "Especially now that I've been repaired."

"Okay!" Bull said. "Can we get this over with? Every minute we wait gets us closer to the deadline."

Gilles clapped like a teacher trying to get their students' attention. "Yes, yes. As amusing as that was, it's quite enough. You are all a team for the rest of the day, so act like it. You don't want to know what happens to you if you don't get that device before time runs out."

CHAPTER 25

When we landed a block from the garage, Gilles's car was the nicest thing by a country mile, and the four of us stuck out like a set of sore thumbs.

Xree patted me on the back. "I just placed a tracker on you. Once you pass through the geofence, I'll activate the jammer, and you have—"

The word 'jammer' caused a lump to form in my throat.

"You okay, mate?"

I took a deep breath. "Yeah, I'm fine."

"You better be on the level," Bull growled. "I am risking quite a bit to be here with you."

"I'm fine."

"Quit blah-blah-blahing and get out of here," John huffed from the driver's seat. "The sooner this is done, the sooner we can get paid and have a shag."

Bull groaned as they exited the car. When they were standing erect, they slammed their chest twice, and their whole body lit up with a thousand little lights that crisscrossed and intersected like a netting. The figure immediately began to morph into an orc with a huge overbite and long tusks.

"Let's go," they said.

I didn't question it. In my line of work, you meet a lot of weird characters with interesting tech; cloaking technology wasn't even the most novel thing I saw that month.

I didn't think seeing the crappy garage we used as a front would have such an effect on me but seeing the neon flashing sign for "Jammer's" sent a wave of emotion through me as we took positions on either side of the alley.

Gilles was right. There were only a couple of officers stationed outside of it, and there was a clear line of sight to the side door, which was closest to the safe that Ballister and Node had told me about.

"You ready?" Bull asked.

I nodded, and they picked up a huge trash can like it was nothing and hurled it toward the door. "Screw you, pigs! Get outta my neighborhood!"

Bull rushed forward toward the cops, who had leaped out of the way of the dumpster. Bull lowered their shoulder and took one of the police off their feet, sending the officer flying into the wall behind them.

"GO!" Xree growled into my ear.

The other officer was distracted by the fight, and when I rushed forward, Bull sprinted away, taking the two officers with them. Even though we took out the video surveillance on the block, I looked up to see the cameras were functional again, so I took to the shadows to make it inside.

"Ready," I said. "Making my move in three, two, one…now."

I pushed open the side door, which had a wonky lock for just this sort of occasion. It made a creak that I tried unsuccessfully to muffle.

"What was that?" a dulcet voice said when I entered the door.

"We're in the Bunghole," another gruffer voice said. "What do you expect? Just keep working, and don't worry about it."

I pushed forward past a worktable until I got a good look at the room. Two people in white coats, each wearing a pair of blue goggles, scanned the walls for something I couldn't imagine. *Were there other secrets Jammer kept from me?* Probably, all fathers hid things from their children.

"Sixty seconds," Xree screeched into my ear.

There was no time for subtlety. The lab coats were in the room where the vault was. In fact, as I scampered closer, they were on either side of it, and it was clear to me they had no idea what they were looking for. I promised Ballister and Node I would play it safe, but this was an emergency.

"Hey!" I shouted.

By the time the two of them turned around, I was on top of them. I punched one in the jaw, knocking them back, and then kicked off to smash the other with a roundhouse to the temple. They weren't soldiers or warriors. Their jaws were glass, and they went down immediately.

"Thirty seconds!" Xree screamed into my ear when I hit the ground.

"I'm going!" I chuffed back.

I looked down at the vault. It was a combination of bio-scanner and facial recognition software. We worked on one just like it a few years ago, and it was impossible to open. Even if you tried and failed, the contents inside would explode. I just hoped that Gilles was right.

I pressed my thumb onto one of my fangs until a dribble of blood came out. I touched it to the bio scan, hoping that it was enough. A moment later, the light under the thumb blinked, and a small porthole in the center of the vault opened. I looked into it as it scanned my face with a laser. This was the moment of truth...

...and a click. The vault unsealed and opened for me. I pulled it open and looked inside. There was a small hard drive, a remote control, and a picture. I picked it up first. It was of me, just a little whelp, playing with a ball of yarn while Jammer looked on lovingly. I didn't even have my cybernetic limbs yet. It must have been just when I came to him.

"Time's up! Get out of there!"

But it was too late to shake me out of my stupor because as I looked down at the picture, a siren started to blare, and red lights flashed from every direction.

CHAPTER 26

I grabbed everything from the vault and slammed it closed. It wasn't just Gilles who wanted what was in the vault, but the police and seemingly everyone else as well. It wasn't clear to me why what my father had was so important, but I was going to figure it out. Jammer was never very forthcoming, but I didn't quite know how many people he was playing against the middle.

I clutched the contents of the vault tightly across my chest as the door swung open, and the two police officers stormed in. They pulled their blasters as I hopped onto the table, and then to the work bench, and then leaped between them and out the door. I tumbled into a roll and popped up into a full sprint without missing a beat.

"Duck!" Bull shouted, still in their orc form. They pulled a phone booth from the ground and tossed it over me. I spun onto the ground as the granite sprinkled over me and then jumped back to my feet to follow them to the car.

"What are you doing here? I thought you were leading them away!"

"They got called back, and then they heard the alarm, and...well, you know the rest."

Xree pushed open the door, and I slid inside. John barely let Bull close the door before he lifted into the air and gunned it. Suddenly, as we moved, the skies were filled with police cruisers every few hundred yards, like they were waiting for us to slip up.

Maybe they were. Maybe Gilles wasn't as connected as they thought, and this was all a set-up from the beginning.

John looked into the rear view at Xree. "Can you do anything?"

Xree typed into her computer. "I'm trying. Turn left here!"

As John spun the wheel, two cars crashed behind us. The lights began to flicker, then went out, and we were driving in darkness. I didn't think much of Xree's ability, but maybe she was a better hacker than I gave her credit for.

"That's kind of impressive."

"Thanks," Xree said. "I always respected your father's work. I studied it when I was on the come-up, so it means a lot you would say that." She clacked onto her keyboard. "Ninety degrees up, NOW!"

John pulled the wheel back and gunned it just as two cruisers descended on our position. "Anyone who relies on autopilot is a wanker."

"You're a genius!" Xree shouted. She started to type furiously on her computer. After a few seconds, she popped her head up. "Watch this."

Her smile broadened as she hit enter and both cars in our path came to a dead stop. With a few more keystrokes, the cars started firing toward the police cars coming at us.

"There!" Bull shouted, pointing to an underpass. John dove down into a ravine. At the far end, a large box truck waited on the side of the bridge as if it had broken down. When they saw John's car, they pulled open the back, and our car slid inside, coming to a stop perfectly as the door slammed closed.

"See, I told you. Nothing to worry about."

"I don't think you said any of that," Xree said to John as he pulled his hands off the wheel. "In fact, you are the tensest person I've ever seen in my whole life."

"That's impossible, love," John replied. "You can't be tense and a good driver at the same time. You gotta be loose as a goose to make good decisions and be clear-headed enough to know that good decisions often look like bad decisions to everyone else but you."

"That explains the jacket, then," Bull said, causing us all to laugh.

"I love this jacket," John said.

"Of course you do," I added. "It's as tacky as you are."

The good spirits continued as we made our way back to Gilles's skyscraper. I couldn't deny I was in a good mood. I never thought I would get into Jammer's safe and find what he left for me, and I only did it with the help of three criminals working for the worst creature in the city.

After sitting in darkness for a short time, the truck came to a lurch, and the back gate slid up. The light collapsed inside, blinding me for a second. When my eyes regained focus, Gilles stood in the hangar. John pulled the car out of the truck, and when it came to a stop, Gilles looked at it.

"It looks perfect, John. I suppose you live to fight another day."

"I told you I was the best, Gilles," John replied. "You just need a little faith."

"Faith, I have," Gilles said. "With you is the issue, but I suppose you have done me a good service, assuming you were successful."

"Of course we were," I said, holding the remote control in my hand. "Here you go."

Gilles smiled and tapped on the button in the center of the remote. When nothing happened, their face soured. "That was anticlimactic. Did it work?"

I shrugged. "I don't kno—"

"Nope," Xree replied, flipping around her computer. On-screen was a countdown clock with less than an hour on it, and the seconds were flipping through faster and faster. "I think you made it mad."

"There's less than an hour left." Gilles turned to me. "Our deal means nothing if this gets out."

"Relax," I replied. "It's all going to be okay. I just need to see my cousins. There's nothing we can't figure out."

"That better be true," Gilles said. "Otherwise, you will be plummeting twenty stories shortly, and there is no way to figure yourself out of that."

CHAPTER 27

"I have no idea how to fix this," Ballister said, looking down at the remote. "I have no idea what it does."

"Maybe this will help," Xree said from across the room.

Against all my better judgment, I allowed her access to my father's hard drive, which she plugged into her computer. I figured it didn't matter much whether somebody else saw it if we were squashed on the asphalt after a twenty-story fall, and it might hold the secret to saving our skins.

I rushed over as she spun the computer around so I could see the monitor. It was Jammer on the screen, though he was considerably young, with none of the gray hair that he developed over the years and only a few of the wrinkles that dotted his face in my memory.

"I hope I've told you this by now, Skritch, but the absolute most important thing you need to do after my death is to reprogram the remote control in this safe to match your DNA instead of mine. It is the only, and I repeat *only,* thing protecting you from Gilles' wrath, and make no mistake, no matter what they say, it is only a matter of time before they kill you if you don't make the swap."

"Yeah, yeah," I replied with words dripping in snark. "I'll remember."

Oops.

What followed was a list of complicated instructions that involved several steps of machining that we could do easily if we had our shop. Ballister and Node watched the video closely, jotting down notes, nodding along, and then silently went to work once the video was done.

"Are you...going to tell Gilles about this?" I asked Xree when the video stopped playing.

Xree sighed. "I don't owe them any favors, but if they offer to pay me for information, then that is my business."

"Then I can assume you are copying that whole hard drive to leverage against them later?"

Xree nodded. "If the rest of the information on this hard drive is a hundredth as potent as what's on that remote control, I'll make a fortune with it."

"No, you won't," I replied. "You'll die, just like Jammer, just like they're trying to do today. I don't know what Jammer has, either, but if he's made a name for himself with Gilles, then he could have been blackmailing any number of people."

"Even better," Xree said. "Then they will pay me to destroy it. Come on, Skritch. Aren't you sick of crawling through air vents and sewer grates to get by? With the information on this drive, we could retire."

"We?" I raised an eyebrow. "And where do you come into this?"

Xree shrugged. "I am currently in possession of the hard drive, and possession is nine-tenths of the law."

I looked back at my cousins. "It's three-on-one in this room."

"Ah, yes, but can you kill me before I wipe the drive clean? Debatable. Then where would you be? Because while your father was supremely talented, he was also a dinosaur. Anything he could do, I can do better. Believe that."

I stared at her for a second, but then I sighed. "All I want off that drive is where to find The Spike and how to figure out where Mouse is hiding. You can have everything else if you help me find that."

"Are you serious?" Xree chuckled. "This is your inheritance. It's possibly worth millions of credits, tens of millions."

"Gotten from pissing off the worst people in this city. I never wanted to do that. I just wanted to do crimes with my pop, and that's been taken away from me."

"I hope you don't expect me to pity you."

"No, I don't expect pity. Empathy would be nice. I know criminal types aren't good about that kind of stuff, me included, so I'll just take your word that you'll help me before you do whatever you do with that stupid hard drive."

Xree nodded. "Fine. I'll even do you one better. I'll save all the sentimental crap off it for you."

"I appreciate that." I stepped forward. "There is just one thing. The location of The Spike...anything about good guys that could be used by bad guys to destroy them...that gets wiped so even you can't find it."

"Are you kidding? That's the most valuable—"

I snapped my fingers. Ballister and Node popped their heads up menacingly. "Three-on-one."

"I could scream."

"I can squeeze pretty hard with this thing." I held up my cybernetic arm. "It's not too much to ask. Be a good guy for once before you go back to being a piece of shit."

Xree smirked. "Flattery will get you everywhere. Very well, I'll help you find The Spike and wipe every piece of identifiable information from this hard drive about your precious good guys...plus, I'll even give you ten percent of the take as a finder's fee."

"That's generous," I turned from her. "But that drive brought my father nothing but an early death. I don't want anything about it. That thing is your curse now."

"Hey!" Ballister shouted. "I think we figured it out."

I walked over to Node as he knelt toward me. The remote control wasn't much to look at, but sometimes, the most important things came in small packages. The remote was little more than a big red button. Pressing it initiated a bio scan of the user. If it matched the information for the user, then it triggered a dead man's switch that reset a counter before a packet got delivered to everyone in the city.

Node flipped a hidden compartment on the side, and a small needle popped out of it. It didn't take a genius to know I needed to poke my finger, which I did. For a moment, the remote flashed to life, and then a light voice said, *"Recognized, Skritch. Counter reset to 48 hours."*

"Now," Ballister said, "according to the video we just watched, you gotta hit that button every 48 hours. You, and you alone. If you don't, then the packets leak."

As if on cue, Gilles opened the door and walked inside. "How are we doing?"

"Well," I said, eyes ping-ponging between the three other creatures in the room. "I have good news and bad news."

CHAPTER 28

"I'm going to kill you," Gilles growled through gritted teeth to me after I explained the situation.

"In fairness," Xree said, "if you do that, then there will be no way to stop the information from getting out."

"And what do I pay you for?" Gilles turned to Xree. "Can't you just go inside the internet and find it?"

Xree stifled a laugh. "You are not very technical, are you?"

"When you have money, you don't need to be. That's why I hire people like you."

Xree jumped down from her chair. "First, you hire me by the job, and you haven't paid me for this one yet, by the way. No worries. I know you're good for it. But second, even if I could find the data you're after, it's probably encrypted ten ways from Sunday with some sort of deadman's trigger that will set it off if I even touch it, which I can't do because the internet is not a physical space you can inhabit, but you catch my drift, right?"

Gilles sneered for long enough I thought their face might have been frozen that way, and then nodded. "Very well, and what happens when Skritch here does something stupid and dies?"

"Whoa, whoa, whoa," I replied. "I have no plans on dying."

"No, but every single bounty hunter in the city, maybe in the whole of the known universe, is after you, and the police are after you as well."

"Then I guess you need to keep me protected." I smiled. "I actually kind of like having a crime boss beholden to me." I held up the remote. "Remember, if I die, you'll be ruined."

"I will find a way to cut your thumb from your hand and synthesize your blood, cat. So, I would be careful with how you speak to me."

"I don't want to talk to you anyway. This might shock you, but I have absolutely no desire to talk to you ever. All I wanted to do was hang out with Pop and commit crimes, but here I am. Now, I'm going to go back to figuring out where to find The Spike and how to find Mouse."

"I regrettably—" Gilles gritted their teeth again "—have information pertinent to that line of inquiry. We have located the woman who acted as the inside man for The Spike's operation. Perhaps she can help you if she is still alive."

"Great!" I said, "If you'll just give me the address, the—"

"If I give this to you," Gilles pulled a piece of paper out of their coat, "then you will be careful, yes?"

I snatched the paper. "Of course, I am always careful. Now, I'm just going to leave this here." I put the remote in front of Ballister and Node. "Remember, you promised to protect them if I helped you, and here I am...helping."

"Your kind of help is the type I never want."

"Back at you," I replied. "However, it looks like we're stuck together."

"It seems that way."

I put the piece of paper in my pocket. "Just out of curiosity, why did you hate my father?"

A wide grin grew on his face. It was not the type of grin that came from laughter but from surreptitious malice. "He really kept you in the dark, didn't he? I thought that maybe this idiot act was all a bluff, but you really don't know?"

"Don't know what?" I shook my head. "If I knew, I wouldn't be asking, would I?"

"Your father was one of my best hackers back in the day, and he was honest, which is not easy to find. When I was on the come-up, everyone was either out to shaft me or kill me, so it was extra impressive that your father was always straight with me. Or...that's how it started, at least, but over time, as the money came in bigger and bigger chunks, I started noticing that money was being skimmed off the top. Even though I had hundreds of creatures working for me and a clear policy of killing anyone who crossed me even a little bit, your father saw fit to use my money to fund an organization meant to bring me, and every criminal in this city, to its knees."

It took a minute for it to connect. "You're talking about The Spike, aren't you?"

"They weren't called that then, but yes. Your father stole ten million credits to fill their coffers, and I have been searching for them ever since. So, you see, if you find The Spike, then I will have found The Spike too... which would be very good for business. I could finally expand beyond the Bunghole if I could show the other crime bosses that I was worthy of—" Gilles cut themselves off and cleared their throat. "Needless to say, he has been persona non grata ever since, hence why he had to construct his elaborate poison pill."

I stepped toward him. "Which begs the question...are you sure you didn't kill my father?"

"Yes!" Gilles replied haughtily. "As you have proven, we are intrinsically tied together. If I wanted him dead, I would have found a way to sever him from his remote connection first. That should be all the proof you need." Gilles pointed to the remote control. "That, and saving your life, because if I really wanted to wound him, we all know that the best way is to hurt his little pet."

"I am not a pet. I was his child."

"Of course," Gilles said. "Isn't that what I said?"

"Okay!" Node shouted. "Since you don't need us right now, can you kindly get out of our office and play missing match on your own time?"

"Yes," Gilles said. "I think that's a decent idea. Ballister, Node, as your cousin has fulfilled her end of the deal, you are no longer confined to this room. I will give you a room in our penthouse for your comfort."

"And what about me?" Xree said.

"You'll be paid, mercenary. Don't worry about that. Then, we will be square until I have future need for your services. Go see the bursar for disbursement."

"You lost my interest after the word 'paid'," Xree said, standing. "But I did hear the word bursar, so it looks like I'll be seeing all of you charming creatures later." Xree bent down and whispered in my ear, "But not too much later, partner."

She placed a piece of paper in my hand and walked out the door. Weird woman, but I hoped she was honest because the person who would probably pay the most for the information on that hard drive was Gilles, and one word from Xree's mouth would get them frothing at the mouth.

So, when she stood and walked toward the door after Gilles, my heart jumped in my throat, and I rushed out after her.

CHAPTER 29

"Hey, hey, hey!" I shouted after Xree as she walked out of the room. "Would you stop for a minute, Xree?"

Xree didn't lose a step as she kept walking in lock step with Gilles. "Why would I stop? Don't you want to track down this lead?"

"I would expect so," Gilles said. "After all, she's been quite a pill about it."

Gilles didn't say another word but continued down the hallway before turning left down another passage. Xree, for herself, kept going down the hallway.

"Are you coming?" Xree asked. "Or don't you want my help?"

I stopped in my tracks. "Uhhh, yeah, I do. But I figured with how quickly you rushed out of the room that you weren't going to help me."

This caused her to stop and turn to me. "Now, why would I forego my big payday?"

I stepped toward her and lowered my voice. "I thought maybe you would just sell everything to Gilles since it's clear he wants information on The Spike, too. You implied you weren't exactly ethical."

"I like money, Skritch." She knelt. "But I hate Gilles more. If they weren't the best-paying crime boss in the city, I would have already turned on them, so the last thing I want is for them to figure out where The Spike is, especially since it riles them up so much."

I scratched my head. "None of that makes sense, Xree, but if you're still going to help me, then let's go."

"That's music to my ears," she replied. "My car is on the street. I hope you don't mind slumming it."

"Are you kidding? Have you seen me? Slumming it is my life."

"Good, because you're gonna get your hands dirty on this one. I can feel it."

The elevator down to the street was filled with silence until we reached the ground, and I found her first-generation hovercar on the street, covered in grime and with multiple scratches and dents along the undercarriage.

"I can see why you wanted to know if I was okay slumming it now."

"See, that's the problem with everything. You look on the outside instead of seeing the beauty underneath the hood. Did you know these first generations are the only ones without a power throttle that prevents you from going more than 200 miles an hour, or that there are no trackers on this model or a way to disable it remotely? Even Gilles's pride and joy doesn't have that. They paid a fortune for it, but I guarantee if the manufacturer wanted to shut it off, they could. That's the problem with all these pretty models.

There is so much tech that big brother can watch. Get in."

She was right. I learned all about them before I infiltrated Gensys. Once they disconnected the computer from their network, about ten thousand cars still on the road would lose their gyroscopics immediately.

The car started with a hum and then a purr. Inside, the car was considerably nicer than on the outside, with brown faux leather seats and a top-of-the-line stereo system that thumped a thick and heavy baseline. As the car rose into the air, I noticed a green light shoot from Xree's hand, and the car shot forward with incredible force.

"You're a wizard," I said to her with a surprised look. I had known wizards to be few and far between, always flashier than anything I had seen from Xree. "Why didn't you tell me?"

"Why would I do that? We barely know each other."

"Because...well..." I stammered. "That's a good point."

"Look, people underestimating me is what has gotten me this far. The fact that I can do almost anything with a computer means I don't have to get into the fray, but when necessary, I can bring the heat, too. It's how I've survived this long."

In the ages before technology, magic had been more important to the natural order of things, but with tech able to replicate nearly anything magic could do, it was less impressive that somebody could manipulate the world with just a thought. Now, you could do that with just about anything you could pick up at a tech store, but having the latent ability to perform magic was a useful skill when all else failed.

"Speaking of..." Xree continued. "You do know that room they kept your cousins was bugged ten ways from Sunday, right? And you just revealed your whole plan in it?"

"I—no, I didn't. Crap. So, how long until—"

"It's hard to believe you lasted this long, but you don't have to worry about it. I jammed their sensors when I got inside. You're lucky I can do that kind of thing on command. Man, Gilles is going to get so angry when he looks at the tape, and it's blank."

"Thank you. You didn't have to do that for me."

"I know," Xree said. "You really don't have to do much for anyone to survive in this world. Learned that the hard way, but I have a good feeling about you. You may be a criminal, but you're not a douchebag like Gilles, and I like that about you."

"You have terrible taste," I laughed. "But thank you."

"Don't thank me yet. Finding The Spike is nearly impossible. They switch servers and locations more than a quantum particle. People have been searching for them everywhere, and yet, they are ghosts. Heck, one could be sitting in front of you right now, and you'd never know."

"That's a weird way to say that. Are you part of The Spike?"

She laughed. "If I were, I definitely wouldn't tell you, Skritch. You're a criminal, after all. I don't trust you as far as I can throw you."

"Well, I am small. You can likely throw me pretty far."

"Just watch yourself, okay?" Xree said. "I won't be around forever, and you're likely to get a laser in the head before the end if you keep acting so recklessly."

"I'll take that under advisement."

CHAPTER 30

The woman lived on the northern end of the city, among the bungalows that most normal citizens couldn't afford. It wasn't the "rich" area of the city, but it was rich-adjacent. These types of houses were filled with sycophants, the types that glommed onto power and enabled bad creatures to be treated as great creatures.

"It's the third one on the left," Xree said as she parked her car across the byway from the house, which had been elevated into the clouds by several platforms, each giving the illusion of space, but they were just fancy brownstones, with a little greenery on them. Bridges connected the brownstones every few homes while at the same time preventing cars from zipping past lest they crash into the zig-zagging structures.

This alone was a luxury not afforded to most, except for those in the bowels of the city. There was a near-constant din of cars zipping past everywhere in the city, and even on the ground, the asphalt reverberated the sound from above.

"I can mask you for ten minutes," Xree said before I left the car. "Any longer than that, and somebody will know you're here, and I can guarantee it will be somebody you don't want to hear from."

There was an eerie silence as I walked across the bridge toward the woman's home. Her name was Ihanma Chilaffa, and she was a typical, boring human. While the city was filled with diversity, the upper echelons of power were almost always human. Sometimes, a token creature or a mutant was allowed inside their ranks. They at least had the same DNA, and it made boards look more diverse than they really were. Usually, those types populated middle management or below—enough power to feel good about themselves but not enough to enact any real change.

She was a senior vice president at Gensys and had been at the company her whole career. Gensys preferred to promote from within, choosing from people already indoctrinated into the company culture and who they could tell were morally flexible. If Ihanma was the mole, though, then perhaps they made a mistake in their recruiting.

Xree already confirmed through a heat map that Ihanma was inside and watching television. She had been home for close to an hour and, according to her calendar, wasn't expecting any company that night. Even without any intel, though, I could see that she was home from the silhouette in the bay window. Most criminals didn't want to be seen committing crimes or exposing themselves as an easy target. Either she was more brazen than others, or she wasn't nearly as evil as her position might suggest.

I knocked on the door with my cybernetic arm. It made a loud, tinny sound against the heavy metal door.

"Go away!" the woman shouted from behind the door. "I don't want any of what you're selling."

"I'm not here to sell you anything, ma'am," I replied. "I'm here to discuss a sensitive matter I don't think you would appreciate getting out into the masses."

"Bribery, is it?" she scoffed. "You must not know who I am."

"Oh, I know who you are," I lied. "And I know where you work, and I know, also, your relation to The Spike—"

I had barely finished my words when the door flung open, and a short, squat human with a mole on the edge of her nose reached forward and pulled me inside.

"You do not say that here. Even the implication—are you trying to get me killed?"

"No, ma'am," I replied. "People have been trying to kill me for a couple of days. I wouldn't wish that on anyone, aside from the one who killed my father."

Ihanma's eyes fell. "You're the cat that tried to break into our systems, then. Yes, I see—"

"I'm a cryptophage, ma'am."

"Of course." She pressed their fingers to the bridge of her nose. "I'm sorry, I've been on edge since—well, you know..."

"I was there. Does that mean it was you who fed—"

She waved their hands in the air. "Don't even say it. It was bad enough once. You know I can neither confirm nor deny anything. They have bugs everywhere."

"I just need to know how to find them. If you can help me find them."

She laughed. "You think I know where they are? They reached out to me, and my life has been a living nightmare ever since. I wake up every day thinking I'm going to get shot in the he—"

And that was when Ihanma's brains splattered across the room, and she collapsed in front of me, dead of a case of dramatic irony.

CHAPTER 31

I barely dodged out of the way of the falling body before three more lasers shot out, breaking through the window and sending more shards of glass along the floor. I ducked under the metal table for protection. The laser beams singed the floor and caused a fire to break out on the carpet, masking my path as I rushed to the door and outside.

A sniper rifle usually had four good charges in it before overheating, which meant I had ninety seconds to find the shooter before they could recharge and reload. From the shape of the holes in the glass, I eyeballed the roofs on the northeast corner of the street. In the darkness, it was hard to make out anything, but the light shifted just enough for me to make out the tip of a hat shake in the cold air.

The assassin must have seen me notice them because the next second, a shadow pushed up from the ground. I leaped onto the bridge and, before I was across it, called out to Xree poking her head out of the hover car. "Meet me on the other side!"

Because of how the bridges crossed the canopy between the buildings, Xree had to make it around the buildings to the west, and if I joined her, I would lose my eye on the shooter. When I was across the street, I leaped onto a ledge and then onto an awning before making my way onto the roof, just in time to see the figure pull up their sniper rifle and rush off into the night.

They weren't satisfied just to kill Ihanma. They took shots at me, too, which meant I was a target as well. How did they know I would be there? The only people who knew I was going were my cousins, who have more to lose from betraying me than anyone...except for maybe Gilles. If I died, everything my father had on him would make its way out into the world. The only other person who knew it was Xree, and she could have shot me at any moment in the car on the way over here. *Why would she betray me now?*

I almost wished it was Gilles or Xree. At least then, there would be a clue to go on instead of this nebulous feeling of dread that followed me everywhere and cast a pall over every relationship in my life.

I leaped from building to building, barely able to keep up with the speed of the assassin, who blended in with the shadows so well it was hard to track them.

"Slow them down," I grunted, opening the latch to my nanites as I rushed forward at top speed.

Nanites weren't usually used to attack people, but they were a great help for infiltrating buildings and getting me into tight spaces, so I figured there was no harm in trying to use them like the cloud that I walked through to sync them with my body.

The nanites shot forward and into the darkness. I felt a pang in my chest watching them go, wondering if I made the right choice and how Ballister and Node would ever trust me again if I destroyed another swarm of their most sacred tech.

It only took a few seconds for me to hear a scream in the darkness and then see four laser beams shoot out, illuminating a figure in the shadows. I gained on them as they stumbled and then heard a clang when their rifle banged against the ground.

"Enough!" I shouted, coming to a dead stop, feet from the assailant. "Drop your weapon, and I'll call them off."

There was a moment of silence, and then a gun fell to the ground with a loud thud. I willed the nanites off the shooter, but they took the form of a long whip that extended from my arm and pulled the gun closer to me.

I never much liked guns or knives. I preferred to use my wits and avoid confrontation as much as possible, relying on the strength of my cybernetic arm and leg to speak for me when words failed. However, I couldn't well let an assassin have easy access to a gun, either.

"Who are you?" I said, stepping forward. "Why are you trying to kill me?"

"Oh, I think you know who I am, Skritch, and as for why I'm trying to kill you—" the figure walked into the light and pulled off her hat "—I think I was clear about that as well...or are you really that thick-headed that you would forget our last meeting?"

"Mouse," I growled, as every molecule of my being vibrated in anger. I gritted and bared my teeth. "I've been looking everywhere for you."

"Oh, I know," she replied casually. "And now you've caught me, cat. What will you do with me now?"

"I'm going to kill you, obviously."

"That worked so well for you last time," she scoffed.

"Now you don't have your guns or your drones. You're defenseless, and I'm prepared for a fight. You won't catch me unprepared again."

She cocked her head to one side. "What makes you think I'm defenseless?"

"Don't be—" my eyes went wide as two drones rose from the far edge of the roof high into the air. Guns trained on me, "—shit."

"Ah, there is the fear I remember. It's incredible how quickly the bravado falls away when we are confronted with our mortality, isn't it?" She smirked. "I was told to keep this quiet, but I don't think my employer will mind much either way, as long as you die in the end. Bye-bye, kitty."

The Gatling guns whirled up on both drones, and every muscle in my body clenched, preparing for the pain of being riddled with bullets.

CHAPTER 32

As my body waited for death, I closed my eyes and took a deep breath. When I opened them, my body relaxed, and everything slowed for a second as I scanned the rooftop for a place to hide. We had made it past the residential housing into an industrial area, which came with an industrial-strength air conditioning unit on the roof to my left. Without thinking, I leaped into the air behind it as the guns unloaded on me.

With my position vacated, Mouse stepped forward and picked up her gun as casually as if she were strolling through the park. "This is the second time you've underestimated me. You won't live to see a third."

Mouse rushed forward, aiming her gun at me as my nanites whipped toward her, knocking the gun out of position as I found another perch. The Gatling guns needed a minute to recharge, which gave me just enough time to leap from one building to the next.

"There's nowhere to hide!" Mouse screamed behind me.

I turned back to see her leap onto her drones and give chase. Even on my new cybernetics, I could not outrun her for long. Even if both of my legs were cybernetic, she would catch me before long, and I was still breaking in everything that my new limbs could do, which gave her an even greater advantage.

I leaped to another building, and when I rose to my feet again, my eyes found that I was running out of real estate. In two more buildings, I would reach the end of the row, as it narrowed into a small peninsula before falling off into the darkness.

I looked back to see Mouse closing in on me. She leveled her sniper rifle and took a shot. I rolled to the right, barely able to avoid the precise aim she had with the weapon. It would have been impressive if it wasn't so terrifying.

I pushed up to my feet and once again leaped into the air to the next building. As I rushed across, a hundred scenarios played out in front of me, but they all ended up with my death, either at the hands of my assassin or plummeting to the ground. My only hope was that somehow Xree would save me, assuming she wasn't the one to call the assassin.

One more leap, and I was at the end of the line. I hoped that I would come up with a perfect plan before I made my final stand, but instead, all I had was a wing and a prayer. I turned back around toward Mouse, waiting for an attack, and sent my nanites flying toward her. It was the only thing that had worked in either of my meetings and if it even gave me a few seconds to come up—

—but as the nanites went to attack, Mouse showed her great flexibility and reflexes as she dodged the cloud completely, bobbing left and then weaving right as the drones maneuvered into their final attack position. The nanites might have another chance to attack, but not before the drones leveled me with their guns.

"Cute," Mouse said. "Now, let's finish this."

"Yes!" I heard Xree scream from behind me. "Let's!"

I turned as the car's shadow crested over me to see Xree leaning over the passenger's seat of the car, firing her blaster through the air. An errant shot hit one of the drones. That sent them into a tailspin as Mouse leaped onto the building, giving the nanites just enough time to return to me.

"Get in!" Xree shouted. "Hurry!"

I didn't need to be told twice. I jumped into the car as Xree pushed up into the driver's seat. The door was barely closed before she gunned it.

"Thank you."

"Don't thank me yet," she replied. "I have a feeling we haven't seen the last of her."

For a moment, I wanted to argue, but when I looked back, I saw she was right. Mouse had jumped onto her singular drone and rushed forward on it, somehow faster than before.

"We're not going to be able to outrun her," I replied.

"Oh no?" Xree smiled. "Watch me."

I had forgotten what Xree said about the speed and maneuverability of her car, so when she slammed on the gas, I was unprepared for the sudden jolt of speed. She spun the wheel as she pulled it back, and we made a ninety-percent nosedive to the left. She zigged and zagged through the traffic masterfully, barely missing cars that shot by in every direction.

My heart pumped in my eyes, and when she stopped, I was sure we had lost Mouse. Only a lunatic with nothing to lose would dare risk something so brazen, but when she pulled up, I looked to the sky to see Mouse right behind us still.

"Who is this woman?" Xree said. "I've never seen anything like her before."

"Yeah, she definitely sucks," I replied. "Can we stop marveling and start getting the heck out of here, though?"

Laser beams shot all around us as Xree gunned it forward through the traffic. "Take the wheel."

She didn't let me answer before she leaned out the window and started to fire at Mouse. I leaned over and pulled the car to the right to level it out as the exchange escalated. Finally, Xree pulled herself back inside and growled.

"This woman will not give up," Xree said. "It's time to do something drastic."

"What does that mean?"

But she didn't answer, except to smile, as she slammed on the brake and spun the wheel. Clearly, Mouse didn't expect a sudden stop because all she had time to do was widen her eyes before she slammed into the car at full force, cracked her head on the door, and plummeted to Earth.

"We need her," I replied.

"You want me to save the woman who was just trying to kill us?" Xree replied in a huff.

"Absolutely."

"I hate you; do you know that?"

"It's a common reaction," I replied. "Now go."

CHAPTER 33

Catching an unconscious woman from the air without breaking all the bones in their body turned out to be a challenge, but it was one that Xree performed with the kind of dexterity that made me wonder if she had done it before.

When Mouse was lying comfortably in the back seat, I turned to her and noticed the relaxed expression of peace on her face. "She doesn't look dangerous now, does she?"

"Don't grow a soft heart now, Skritch. You'll need an icy one for what happens next."

That raised my eyebrow. "What are we doing now?"

"You'll see." Xree didn't break the cold expression on her face. "I think it's time you met my friends."

Though I peppered her with questions during the rest of our trip, she refused to answer them. Instead, she simply turned up the radio with every word from my mouth until I couldn't even hear myself think. I could tell the pain on her face, but she clearly thought it was less painful than answering my questions.

It surprised me that Mouse did not wake up with the shrieking coming from the speakers, along with the rumbling bass I was worried would shake the feeble car until it fell apart. Still, after an agonizing fifteen minutes, we came to a stop in front of a black metal building squeezed between two massive structures. You could have lost it in the shadow of the others if you weren't looking for it, and even knowing what to look for, I could barely make it out.

"Wait here and watch her."

Xree didn't wait for a response before she left the car and disappeared into the building. I was not used to taking orders, and there were way too many of them for my liking. Still, it was hard to argue with the results. We found Mouse together, and soon, I would get answers.

Five minutes later, Xree stormed out of the building with two burly orcs who looked not to be trifled with. Even for muscle, they seemed angry and unapproachable.

"Get her out the back." There was a silence as the two looked back at her. "You've made your opinion known, and I'm telling you to do it. Don't make me get Dotty on you."

The orcs grumbled but did as they were told. Mouse was like a ragdoll as they pulled her out of the car, and I wondered if she would ever wake up again. After the orcs were clear of the car, Xree beckoned me to join her, and we walked inside. For the sleek exterior, the inside of the building was covered in stickers and reeked of must. Dozens of creatures speckled the large room in the center.

"This way." Xree's eyes moved to the orcs. "Get her into room four and stabilized. Restrain her, and don't let her out of your sight. She's a slippery one."

They nodded begrudgingly, and I followed Xree up the industrial metal stairs. The second floor had a black concrete floor and six decks. All manner of creatures sat on them, punching their keyboards as if they owed their operators money.

We continued up the stairs to a large silver door adorned with stickers and murals, the same aesthetic as the rest of the building, but instead of passing through without stopping, Xree stopped in front of it and turned to me.

"Listen closely to me," Xree said. "If you speak a word to anyone about anything you see behind this room, we will find you, and we will kill you. Do you understand? My friends are very helpful and very secretive."

I nodded. "I won't say anything. You have my word."

"You might not think I take a lot of stock in the word of thieves, but at least you're honest about bilking people out of money. I respect that. I think you and Dotty will get along."

Xree typed a code into a keypad and then muttered a spell that made the whole door glow green. Once the spell dissipated, the doors opened into another large room that looked like the deck of a spaceship. In the center of the room was a large console with ten monitors.

The chair at the center of the console spun, and the most beautiful android I had ever seen stood. Instead of metal, they were made of white porcelain engraved with flowers, and every joint glowed a beautiful, haunting blue with each step.

"Welcome back, Xree."

"Good to see you, Dotty," Xree replied. "I wish it was under better circumstances."

Dotty nodded slowly. "I understand that, but the nature of our business is so dangerous that making it back home is always a cause for celebration. Do you have it, then?"

Xree nodded and pulled her laptop out, along with the hard drive that my father left for me. "It's all right here."

"Good," Dotty said. "You have done well, Xree."

"Hey!" I shouted. "What the hell is going on here? That is mine!"

I rushed forward, and Dotty took a step back, clapping two hands that had, until this moment, been hidden inside her chassis. As she moved back, a forcefield rose, separating us.

"We can't have this kind of outburst, Skritch." Dotty moved forward again, now protected by the forcefield. "This information was the price of your admission to our base. If you behave, you will be initiated into our ranks and have access to more information that you could inject for the rest of your life."

"I don't care. I'm not here to join your club. I'm here to find The Spike and figure out who put out a hit on my father."

"Skritch, you big dummy. This is The Spike, and Dotty is its founder. Show some respect, why don't you?" Xree explained, rolling her eyes.

CHAPTER 34

"Excuse me?" I blubbered out, confused. "You're saying you're the infamous Spike that has been terrorizing corporations and bad guys for years?"

Dotty cocked her head. "Not by myself. We have a collection of talented freelancers and volunteers who do much of the work for us, but I am responsible for the security, safety, and anonymity of the organization." She stepped up to the edge of the force field. "I would like to lower this forcefield now, but to do that, I need to know you have calmed down."

I blinked several times, trying to process the information I had been handed. "If you really are The Spike, then I'm not mad at you. Of all the organizations in this terrible city, you are one of the least terrible I've come across."

"Thank you." Dotty lowered the shield. "The modulation of your voice tells me both that you have calmed down and are telling the truth, which makes me very happy."

I cocked my head back at Xree. "Why all the secrecy though?"

"We do not offer entrance to our base lightly," Xree said. "I have been following you since your father's death, trying to find ways to help you and help decide whether you were worthy of joining us."

"Of course, you must understand," Dotty said. "The utmost secrecy is needed to keep our operation underground. While this building is equipped with stealth and flight capabilities—"

"Wait. This building can fly?"

"That's right," Dotty replied. "How do you think we've remained hidden so long?"

"I don't—"

"By moving from place to place. Still, there are only so many places to hide in this town, and over the years, the safe harbors have become fewer and further between."

"Yes," I said with a nod. "I can imagine you've pissed off a lot of people in your day. I only know a small list of them."

Dotty stayed silent for a second, like she was lost in thought. "I count 368 organizations which we have ousted from power or exposed as frauds. However, even with all that, it is only a small fraction of a fraction, like throwing a rock into an ocean. The immediate area around the rock ripples for a moment, but then the water grows still again, and the ocean hasn't even noticed what you have done to it."

"That is a bleak image you paint," I said.

"It is bleak," Xree replied. "And the more companies we bring down, the more cautious the others get, and the more money they spend bringing us down. We have our funding sources, but they dry up quicker these days than ever before."

"Like my father," I said, eyes filling with tears until I wiped them away. "He helped fund your startup costs, right?"

Dotty nodded slowly. "He was a great supporter of ours until the end. It truly is a tragedy what the world does to good people. He is one of many that we have lost over the years. We have operatives all over the known universe, and they funnel us money when they can. It is dangerous work and growing more dangerous over time."

"Well, how can I help?" I asked confidently. "If my father believed in you, then I do, too. He said you would have the best chance of figuring out who killed him and who is trying to kill me."

Dotty's glowing eyes shut for a long moment and then opened again. "We have several possibilities, of course, but your father was wrong...the best chance for you to find out who killed your father is to ask the assassin who set you up. We can make our assumptions, of course, and trace where we can, but it is long, arduous work." She paused. "In fact, we have been working on it since we heard the news, and every trail leads to a dead end. Whoever did this, they don't only have hackers and security firms working on it, but several high-level wizards protecting their trails."

"Like Xree?" I asked.

Xree chuckled. "Way more powerful than me, but I appreciate the comparison. These wizards...the things they can do, I've never even thought about trying until I was way more powerful."

"Then, I suppose the only thing to do is interrogate Mouse and try to find a way for her to break."

"We have ways," Xree said. "But it is messy work, not for the faint of heart."

"Mouse killed my father." I took a deep breath to steel my resolve. "I want her to suffer. If it helps us break her, I'm more than okay with that."

"Don't let your emotions cloud your judgment," Dotty said. "The reason I am in charge is because everything I do is dictated by reason and logic. Emotions cause us to act rashly and make mistakes. We live on the edge of a razor, a Sword of Damocles hanging over us. Any false movement and we risk annihilation."

"I will not be reckless," I replied. "I am used to high-stress situations."

"Good," Xree said. "I think it would be good to have you in on the interrogation. You clearly have a rapport with this assassin. Maybe bringing you into the room will make her slip up and make a mistake."

"I have been known to get under people's skin. If I can be of help, then please, use me any way you need."

"You are a good one," Dotty said. "Your father spoke of you often, and it is nice that his faith in you was justified."

I bit my lip. "I am upset that my father didn't feel comfortable telling me more about you, but I am very glad I can continue his work with you. I think that would make him happy, that I continue his legacy."

"I agree, young Skritch," Dotty said. "I am sure you will do him proud."

CHAPTER 35

Xree motioned for me to follow her as Dotty went back to work. We left the command center. I followed her down to the level below before she stopped and turned to me.

"Have you ever interrogated somebody before?" she asked. "Because it's not as simple as just talking or punching."

"I'm more of a finesse criminal. I don't do much hard-hitting or psychological warfare."

She started walking again. "I thought as much. Interrogation is as much a battle of wills as anything else. Good interrogators can catch somebody in a lie by peppering them with enough questions and making sure a conversation doubles back on itself smoothly, leaving the perp confused and liable to make a mistake. Mouse is not just a simpleton who will break easily. She's a trained assassin, which means she'll understand our tricks and use them to her benefit. That is where you come in."

"How do you know this?"

"I've led a long and fruitful life before you. I know I come off as a hacker, but I've been a spy for years, slipping into and out of costumes as easily as you put on socks."

"I don't wear socks, what with the fur and all."

"It was a turn of phrase," she said with a sigh.

"I've never heard it before, and it's not a very good one even if I had, is it?"

She pointed at me. "This is what we need in there. Be exactly this annoying, and we'll be sure to break her. I don't know anyone who can resist getting infuriated at your stupid banter."

"You got it, boss," I said, giving a little sarcastic salute.

"I'm not your boss yet," she said with a smirk that turned into a grimace. "And if you keep this up, I'll make sure I never will be. Save it for the interrogation."

We reached the bottom floor, and Xree turned left, stopping in front of a big metal door with the two orc guards stationed in front of it. "Is she ready?"

One of the orcs nodded. "Doc says she's stable, and we got her on a drip. Should be kicking in every minute."

"What's in the drip?" I asked, sidling up to Xree.

"It's a potent truth serum. With normal ding-dongs it works in a matter of minutes, but I'm sure that Mouse has worked to build up an immunity to it, so all I expect is for it to give us the edge. What happens in there is on us, you and me, and how we work as a team, got it?"

I nodded. "Got it."

The orcs opened the metal door, and we entered a dark room. There were little more than a couple of lights coming from the medical equipment in the room, and it was silent except for the beeping of a monitor on the other side of the room. When we entered, the lights came up throughout the room, revealing Mouse in a bed, staring at us with a deep scowl.

"Thanks for that. The darkness was driving me crazy."

"We hope it gave you a chance to think," Xree said. "Maybe give a second thought to the company you keep."

Mouse's head listed from side to side, looking slightly drunk, before turning her attention to me. "I could say the same for you, kitty."

"I'm not a—" My eyes narrowed. "We're not the ones who kill people for a living."

"Is that true?" Mouse's neck rolled until she was addressing Xree. "What name do you go by these days? Neruda? Or is it Xhimo? It's so hard keeping track of your different personalities."

"It's Xree," she replied. "I wish I could say it was good to see you again, Melita."

"You...know her?" I asked, confused.

"Unfortunately," Mouse said. "We grew up together. Or should I say when we were on the come-up together on the streets of Zhakatal."

It was hard to keep my heart from bleeding from the wound I felt growing in my chest. "You knew about this, and you didn't tell me?"

"It was need to know," Xree said. "Besides, I wasn't sure it was her until she slammed into my car. Age has not been kind to her."

So many things floated through my mind. I immediately started to wonder if I could trust the goblin next to me or anything I had heard since showing up at The Spike's headquarters. There was secrecy, which I understood, then there was manipulation, and I began to feel like I was being manipulated.

"Isn't it funny?" Mouse said. "You think you know somebody, and then they turn on you. It's a feeling I know well, little cat."

"Enough!" Xree shouted, stepping forward. "This is not about me. It's about you. Tell me, Melita. Who hired you to kill Skritch's father?"

Mouse rolled her head around for a long, luxurious minute. "I forgot what Geppa felt like, but when you're on it, there's nothing like the feeling. You forget the world, and your head feels like it's about to float off your body. I absolutely love it."

"Stop changing the subject," I growled. "Who hired you?"

"This is a tactic. When you are confronted with a question that could incriminate you, change the subject." Xree reached forward and grabbed Mouse's leg, squeezing the left calf tightly. "Focus on me, Melita. Who hired you?"

"There are so many answers to that question. You were never good at this part. I'm surprised you survived so far because when the rubber meets the road, you fall apart. No wonder you haven't found me yet."

"But I found you." I leaped onto the bed, and my cybernetic leg clawed into Mouse's skin. "Why did you kill my father?"

"Cuz it was a job, love. I had no ill will toward him. Now, you, on the other hand, are a nuisance. I will kill you for free, eventually, out of the goodness of my heart."

"Hey!" Xree shouted. "Stop insulting her, and let's get back to the order at hand. Who hired you to kill Jammer? If you get off task again, I will cut your foot off at the shin and let you bleed out."

"So hostile," Mouse said. "After everything we've been through, do you really think I would tell you anything?"

"I don't think you'll have a chance in a second. We pumped you full of enough Geppa to kill an elephant. Either you'll tell us, or you'll die."

"That wasn't the plan," I said. "She can't die. Not until I have what I need."

Xree narrowed her eyes at me as if I caused some great slight against her, but it was Mouse who replied to me. "Don't worry, little one. You will have your revenge. If you are brave enough to take it is another matter."

"What does that mean?" I asked.

"I am a businesswoman," Mouse said. "If you want information, it will cost you. My lips will stay sealed, and maybe I will die, unless you pay me ten million credits."

"Ten million!" Xree shouted. "You must be out of your mind."

Mouse shook her head loosely. "I never kid about money. That will get me off-planet and able to start a life far away from this terrible city, along with the ability to buy the power I need to keep myself protected and never work again."

"Or we can give you more Geppa until we find a lethal dose."

"You should know I don't fear death. I have watched the light fade from enough marks that I have become close with it. Some days, I even wish for it."

"We don't have that kind of money," I said.

"Well, aren't you a thief?" Mouse asked. "Maybe you can steal it. Either way, look into my eyes and realize the truth; I would rather die than help you any other way."

"This is useless. Come on, Skritch," Xree said. "I think we need to regroup and come up with another plan."

"Oh, yes, please," Mouse said. "I do so love being chased by you again, Neruda. It reminds me of the good old days. Though, they weren't all they were cracked up to be either, were they?"

CHAPTER 36

Xree punched a hole into the black wall after we exited the room, breaking a sticker of a rat in half and sending it through the wall.

"What happened in there?" I said. "I thought we had a plan, and it all fell apart—"

"No plan survives first contact with the enemy." She turned to me. "You might have noticed she and I have a history..."

"Yeah...it came up. What is up with that?" I asked. "You make a habit of hanging out with murderers?"

"When I was coming up, yeah." She scratched her head. "We both grew up on the streets. Neither of us was lucky enough to have a father like Jammer looking out for us, and the orphanage the city stuck us in would rather have sold us into slavery to a passing galley than lift a finger to help us. So we left and figured it out on our own. It sucked, but we made it through until we were teenagers. That's when we met Fabian Zchar and fell in with his crew back when they were on the come-up."

The Zchar family. I hadn't thought of them much in my life, but this was the second time they came up in the last two days. The first was when I helped Vazia Zchar escape prison, and now, there was this connection. It felt like too much of a coincidence not to mean anything.

"So, you were criminals."

"I'm still a criminal, Skritch," Xree said. "I just work for the good guys now, but back then, I didn't care. I had no morals; I couldn't afford them. I was too hungry and broke for morals, so I did some things I wasn't proud of, and so did Melita. She took to it like an old hat. The streets taught her a…moral flexibility that allowed her to compartmentalize the terrible things the Zchars asked her to do. Meanwhile, I found out I had some affinity for computers and magical things of a certain sort, so I fell behind a computer. I thought since I couldn't see the people I was hurting, they didn't exist, but eventually, that kind of thing catches up with you."

"Yes." The words she spoke hit me hard. "I used to justify my thefts because I couldn't see who I was hurting."

"Jammer and I were alike like that, too. We bonded over the fact that the razor's edge we walked didn't sit well with us. I'm not surprised as his kid that you found the same thing in your work."

"Maybe," I said wistfully.

"Me too," she replied. "Dotty showed me that I could help people instead of hurting them, and that resonated."

"Maybe the Zchar family is responsible for all of the stuff that's happened to me."

"I don't think so. This isn't their speed. They steal from the police and sell to criminals. They don't—"

"It's the best lead we have," I said. "Unless you have ten million credits lying around."

"Well, not lying around," Xree chuckled. "However, it's literally our thing to find money and…reappropriate it for the cause, so I'm sure we could find the money. I'm not sure Dotty will go for it, though. She has a thing about negotiating with criminals."

"Just show her the logic behind doing so." I stepped toward the door. "Meanwhile, I'm going to see what I can dredge up on the Zchar family. Maybe there's a connection there we're not seeing."

"What are you going to do? Walk in the front door?"

"I have my ways," I said. "Besides, Vazia Zchar owes me a favor, so the least they can do is look me in the eyes before they drain the life out of me."

"You're crazy. Did you know that?" Xree said.

"I've been told that a time or two before." I sighed. "I'll be as careful as I can. I'll wait until Vazia is alone before I confront them, but I can't just sit here on my hands, and this is the best lead we might get."

"No, you're right," Xree said. "I've just grown to like you since we met, so go dying or anything, alright?"

"I'll do my best."

CHAPTER 37

This was stupid, and I knew it was stupid, but I couldn't shake the fact that something was off. I felt too uneasy to rest until I got to the bottom of it. Yes, there was certainly a mercenary quality to Mouse's offer, but she didn't seem like the type to go into hiding or sell out her clients for money, even if it was a lot of money.

The Zchar family might not give me any clues, but it would hopefully illuminate the past of not just Mouse but Xree as well, all while letting me clear my head. There was something I was missing about their connection, and I couldn't rely on either of them to tell me the truth.

There was a secondary reason for visiting Vazia Zchar. I was mercilessly low on friends, and I could use as many as I could get right now. It was unclear if they would even remember me, but I hoped with a little time, I could remind them what I had done to free them from the police station.

It wasn't hard to find the Zchar compound. Unlike The Spike, the Zchars committed crimes out in the open, and unlike Gilles, they were strong enough to fight off any challenge. Honestly, I wondered how any of them were captured, given that you rarely saw Vazia outside the compound, which was in the richest area of the city. Unlike the brownstones where I confronted Mouse, which used interconnected pathways to deter hover cars from entering their area of the city, New Town paid security professionals to barricade the city from unwanted intruders.

Of course, being the sneaky sort, it wasn't hard for me to slide past their security gates and into the massive hillside space where the richest families in the city lived. The security guards were easy to fool on the way in. After all, they were looking for cars and trucks, not small cryptophages that could blend in with their surroundings and disappear.

Most of Zhakatal was built on a natural gulch, but New Town was built on a hill that naturally overlooked everything else not on it and had the two things the rest of the city desperately lacked: privacy and vegetation. Sure, some of the city buildings featured hanging gardens, and many of the residents grew herbs on their balconies if they were lucky enough to have them, but there was no land to dig into except in New Town. While 99% of our food was produced inside artificial greenhouses, the estates in New Town ate from vegetables and fruit harvested from the very ground itself.

The smell of flowers bloomed in my nose as I slid from house to house. It overpowered the terrible, acrid smell of batteries and car exhausts that permeated most of the city and left a pall on just about everything that it touched.

The Zchars did not hide except behind the walls of their compound. Their house rested on one of the highest parts of the hillside, with a huge Z made of gold emblazoned on top of the gates.

It was an artifact of a simpler time. Gates were, especially in a world that could move in three dimensions, irrelevant and were only for aesthetics. I opened the hatch to my nanites, and they quickly found the forcefield encompassing their whole complex.

Luckily, I was prepared and pulled out a matter disrupter from a small rucksack I recovered from a hiding place Jammer kept throughout the city in case we ever needed them. Up until now, I hadn't had a chance to think about them, but it was good planning on his part.

The nanites wrapped around the matter disrupter and placed it on the security shield. It was a good thing the forcefield was made from tech and not magic; otherwise, this would never work. When the device was placed, I pressed the button at the center and a small quake disrupted the shield long enough for me to sneak inside the small hole that it created. The nanites just pulled the matter disrupter through before the shield collapsed behind us again.

I slipped the device back into my sack and pulled out a set of suction cups, which helped me gain purchase on the wall and allowed me to climb it easily. On the other side of the wall, I stuffed the rucksack into a bush and disappeared behind the greenery that lined the compound. I passed glittering pools and water fountains depicting dolphins that spat water into the air.

Most actual houses were sparse in the city, but these were not only spacious but loaded with stuff: bushes, trees, ledges, crevices, and more. It was a thief's dream and made it a breeze to sneak up to the main house.

The main house was made not of metal like everything else in Zhakatal but brick and mortar, which made climbing it easy. Security often breeds a false sense of bravado. When you pay a lot for security, you tend to stop looking over your shoulder, and when blind spots emerge, they grow into holes wide enough to drive a semi-truck through.

The Zchars' compound was no exception. While I saw soldiers and guards marking the complex, they clearly had not seen battle for a long time and had grown complacent in their job, which allowed me to scale the wall and find an open window.

Now, it was just a matter of—

Click. Something moved on the other side of the room. When they stepped into the light, it was Vazia, holding a laser gun pointed at my chest.

"I was wondering when you would come," they said. "Shame I have to kill you now."

CHAPTER 38

"Are you serious?" I said, throwing my hands in the air. "I can't even with this crap today. I saved your life, and you're pointing a gun at me!"

Vazia smiled. "Most people beg for their lives right about now."

I placed my hands on my hips. "Well, those people haven't seen what I've seen. So, you know what? Go for it. Shoot me if that's what you have to do. I literally do not care anymore. This is what I get for trying to—"

Vazia slid their gun back into her belt. "Okay, enough. If there's one thing I can't stand, it's a whiner."

"Wait...you aren't going to kill me?" I asked. "Then what is all this for?"

"You trespassed into my house," they said. "Wouldn't you kill you if you were me?"

"Maybe, or maybe I would think I was the enterprising sort and—" I shook my head. "Can we cut the charades and hypotheticals? I'm glad you aren't going to kill me because I really need to talk with you."

They beckoned me forward. "Come with me."

I followed them out of the room and into the palatial hallway adorned with paintings and filled with plants. It was the exact opposite of everything I had seen in my life, except for in pictures. Even museums devoted to the past didn't have this kind of opulence.

"I want to thank you for letting me out. I understand it wasn't part of your plan, but I appreciate it anyway, even if it was just an ancillary effect."

"It's good to see you were able to escape. I thought for sure you would be recaptured."

"Well, I was planning my own escape, and the two just happened to align and save me quite a bit of time." Vazia started down a marble staircase. "Of course, it was nice to show the police who was really in charge."

"I expect since you were in jail, it means you don't control the police, then."

"Some of them, sure, but not all. Most of my work is done on the fringes, where they won't miss a few million dollars of stolen tech. Of course, that puts me at odds with the other families and the police more times than not. I figure, if the police can be equipped like an army, the least we can do is be equally prepared."

"Do you know who had you arrested?" I asked, suspecting it was the same being that had me arrested. "Because I think they put a hit out on me."

They shook their head. "It could have been any of the families or even somebody in my own employ. There are dozens of options. We're doing a deep dive into our organization right now, but so far, all our efforts have come up fruitless."

I growled. "There's a lot of that going around today."

"Make no mistake, when we find the culprit, and we will find them, I will make an example of them that will turn your stomach."

Vazia and I finished descending the stairs and they led me through the front of the house, with higher ceilings than any warehouse I had ever seen, and into a dining room with a large wooden table in it. Wood was at a premium in the city, and seeing it used in such an impractical way, as decoration, was comical to me.

"I would prefer to take tea in the atrium." Vazia clapped their hands. "Do you like tea?"

"I've never had tea," I replied.

"Oh, you're going to love it. Farhan makes it with these little cucumber sandwiches, which are just lovely." We continued through the kitchen, where they stopped in front of a tall snake cryptophage with bright blue skin. "Add another cup, and we'll take our tea outside if you don't mind."

"You have escaped prison and are taking tea with a known criminal while you are also wanted by the police?" the butler said. "Are you sure that is wise?"

"Yes, I am. I will not live in fear, and I like tea, especially when there are big things to ponder." Vazia's eyes narrowed. "Do you think it is wise to argue with me?"

"Not at all, Mx."

They continued through the kitchen and into the backyard. What struck me, aside from the fragrant smell, was the light that came from every direction. It always seemed like night in the city, what with the large buildings that blotted out the sun, but here, light seemed to stream in from everywhere all the time.

Vazia reached a large glass building simply brimming with green leaves and pushed the simple glass open. Inside, there were hundreds of trees I had never seen before. They pulled a red berry off a small bush and gushed over how delicious it was. Then, they turned around and offered me one. I couldn't resist, and as the juice squirted into my mouth, I thought it must be the most delicious thing I had ever tasted.

"Better than the muck they feed in the city, right?" Vazia said.

"Totally," I replied. "I've heard of greenhouses but never been inside a natural one. I never thought I would see the day."

"That is horrible. I hate that story." Vazia plucked a berry off a bush. "I don't even think they could grow a raspberry if they tried."

They continued into the center of the room, where a small table had been set up to catch the sun. They took one of the chairs and gestured for me to sit down.

"It's like you knew I was coming," I said.

"There are only so many places for you to run, and I figured once you ran out of other places, you would end up here, begging for a favor, thinking I owed you something. The incursion on our shield and the clumsy way you meandered through our compound was confirmation of that."

"Clumsy?" I asked, offended, as the butler placed tea and sandwiches in front of us both. "That is just about the most offensive thing you can say to me."

"Besides calling you a cat, of course," they said with a smirk. "Don't worry. I would never do that. I hate when people insult me like that, too."

"Do people call you that still?"

"Less so now. It helps to run a huge criminal enterprise with a reputation for killing people who slight me."

"Ah, so that's what I was doing wrong, then."

Vazia took a triangle of a sandwich and took a bite. "Mmm, mmm, mmm. So, tell me all about your adventures since we parted ways, and then I will see if I can help you."

"It all started with a Mouse..." I began.

CHAPTER 39

"Well..." Vazia said, sipping their tea. "That's quite a story, and I assume you are here because you think I have some great insight as to Melita and Neruda?"

I dropped my head. "I don't know what I wanted. What I want is to figure out who is trying to kill me and kill them first."

"It seems like you have your answer in Melita...or Mouse, as you call her, then. Why not just kill her?"

I eyed them closely. "The fact you can say that with a straight face, knowing how much she did for you over the years, is eerie."

"She left years ago to go out on her own. I wished her well, but she knew the risks. This business comes with a certain amount of detachment, even for those you have known most of your life." They took another sip. I still hadn't touched mine in case it was poisoned. "But I don't think you will kill her, which is another reason I can be confident in keeping myself detached." Vazia scrunched their face, deep in thought. "You are sure she said ten million credits?"

"It's not the type of number you forget quickly," I said.

"Interesting." Vazia sucked their teeth. "When she was young, and both of them were in my employ, they used to talk about leaving the city and starting over in another system. They had a plan and everything. Any idea how much money they said they needed?"

It couldn't be. "Ten million credits?"

They nodded. "You are very smart for a dumb thief."

I scratched my chin and thought for a moment. "Then…do you think it was a signal to Neruda, Xree, whatever her name is, like an elaborate grift?"

Vazia shrugged. "I don't know what it means. I only know it happened."

"But what reason would they have to try and kill me?" I asked. "I never did anything to them."

"I don't know why. I only know that." Vazia shrugged. "Maybe they thought I would kill you, then they wouldn't have to deal with it. You gave Neruda that hard drive, right? Maybe she does plan on selling it to the highest bidder and needed to get everyone else out of the way first. We're just speculating, though. If you want to check it out, I can get a driver to bring you back across the city."

I chuckled. "I don't think it's a good idea to show you where I'm going."

"I appreciate your caution." They put down their tea. "Of course, if I really wanted that information, I could torture you for it."

"Uhh—"

"But I won't do that. Consider it my favor to you. Now, our debt is repaid. I suggest you get out of my sight, though, before I change my mind."

I didn't argue. You don't argue with people like that. I heard stories about Vazia's whims changing on a dime, and I didn't want to be anywhere in their vicinity when it did. I found my rucksack and made my way back over the wall. It wasn't hard to make it back across the city, but it took seven buses, three switchbacks, and multiple disguises to prevent me from being clocked as the most wanted creature in the city.

None of this sat well with me, but I thought I would get some insight from Vazia that could aid me in tracking down the people trying to kill me. Before I left, Xree told me it was a waste of time, but she needed time to pull together the money, and I wasn't ready to wait for my future to be decided for me.

Did I really think Vazia would, what, lend me ten million credits? Point me in the right direction? Confess to wanting to murder me themselves? Those were the idiotic ideas of a child, and I grew out of those years ago. The minute your parents died, no matter the age, you became an adult, in spirit if not in the eyes of the law.

I wished I could talk to Jammer one last time so he could tell me what to do and show me what I was missing because I had a feeling it was staring me right in the face, mocking me, and I was too blind to see it, or maybe too naïve to see it.

I was five blocks away from the hideout when I smelt the fire cutting through the air. The billowing smoke came next, pluming like a tire fire as dozens of people started to gather around, staring at the burning building. The Spike's headquarters was on fire, and I knew in my bones it had something to do with me. There are no coincidences, and even if I didn't know why, I at least knew that.

CHAPTER 40

It didn't take more than a few seconds for my eyes to track four drones through the billowing smoke. My initial instinct was Mouse had found a way to escape, and now I was more than sure of it. However, with the drones close, I was confident she was still inside, and I had a chance to end this once and for all.

I rushed inside the building as smoke and fire spilled out. The one thing that separated us last time was that I had a desire to live, but now we were on equal footing because I truly didn't care if I died as long as she came with me.

The scene inside was a massacre. No longer were hipster hackers clacking away at their keyboards, but they now lay on the ground in pools of their own blood. The two orc bouncers who brought Mouse inside the base were now riddled with bullets, one on top of the other.

I didn't know what compelled me to look in the cell where Mouse once was, but a quick inspection of it saw the restraints cut and a nurse lying bloody on the floor, their throat slit and eyes cloudy.

"Help!" I heard the plea cut through the cracking fires that raged outside. I rushed back outside and heard the scream again coming from above me. I leaped up the stairs until I reached the second floor. It was more of the same as I saw below, and I surprised myself with how quickly I anesthetized myself to the look of blood and dead bodies. It was sad, of course, but I was on a mission.

"Help!" The voice screamed more forcefully this time, and I rushed to the back of the room to find Xree lying in a pool of her own sick; a heavy beam had fallen over her.

"Stay still!" I shouted, calling forth my nanites until they plumed up into a long rope. I used our combined force to pull the beam enough for her to find freedom and then allowed it to collapse back to the ground. "Are you okay?"

"I don't think I'll ever be okay again, but I think I can walk." She moved forward and then collapsed on the ground. "Maybe not."

"Where is Mouse?" I asked.

"Upstairs. It was horrible, Skritch. She found a way out of her restraints and recovered her gear. After that, it was a simple matter of calling her drones to her, and we were sitting ducks. The defenses barely had a chance to spin up before we were overrun. I tried—I tried to stop her, but she forced me to open Dotty's room, and by that time, the fire ate into the ceilings, making them soft, and I fell."

"Come on," I said, using my nanites to help pull her along up the stairs. "And be careful."

It was harder to move up the stairs slowly with the unbearable heat underneath me, but there was no other choice. I didn't know what Mouse was after, but I couldn't let her take it.

"Can you open it?" I said when we finally reached the top of the stairs. The door was closed in front of us, and she went to open it.

She pressed her hand on the pad like she had before, but even after she used her techno-magic, it wouldn't budge. "Melita must have added more protection. I need to use your nanites to get this door open. I think, with them, I can overwrite it."

"Of course. Take what you need."

A small smile crested on her face as she nodded and worked the nanites into the pad. It took a couple of seconds, which felt like years, but then I heard the lock click and the door swing open. Inside, Dotty turned to Xree from her command console and then down to me.

"Oh, Skritch, what have you done?" Dotty said.

"What are you talking about?" I said. "I'm here to save you."

"I think she's talking about me." I turned to see Mouse leap down from the ceiling to the door, five drones following behind her. "Thanks for the assist, kitty. We have been trying for over a year to get Dotty's guard down so we could slip inside, and we really couldn't have done it without you."

"Sorry about this, Skritch," Xree said. "I had hoped Vazia would keep you busy until we were gone, but it turns out you are more useful alive than dead. Still, can't have you interfering until we're done."

Xree kicked me across the room before I could defend myself, and I slid down the wall, barely hanging onto consciousness.

"I can't let you do that," Dotty said, extending all four of her arms and rushing forward to fight them. Metallic weapons extended from them, long, sleek, and deadly, and for a moment, there was hope in my heart.

Dotty destroyed two of the drones, but the swarm fought back, firing a dozen laser blasts into her chassis until it was too much for her. Seeing weakness, Mouse closed in, dismantling one of her arms and drawing the full weight of her attention.

"Quit messing around!" Xree said, sliding into position at the console, and it started Dotty to turn. It was as if Mouse was toying with the porcelain android because, with the command, she took a sword from her back and sliced Dotty through.

"You really should have been made of stronger stuff," Mouse said as Dotty slid down, in two parts, to the ground.

"Don't let her move," Mouse said to the remaining three droids, pointing at me. She walked through the room, and the forcefield rose, cutting them off from the fires raging in the rest of the room. As the drones wound up their guns, I got déjà vu; I had been there before, waiting to be killed by Mouse's drones. She had underestimated me for the last time.

CHAPTER 41

I slapped on a stimpatch and leaped off the wall onto the first drone, cutting through it before I jumped to the second.

I unleashed my nanites and whipped at the third drone. I wrapped them around one of its arms and swung it into the wall, where it crashed through and was consumed by the fire. I took the moment of respite to smash through the chassis of the second drone and pulled out as many wires as I could grab. The drone started to spin out of control just as the third drone made its way through the fire, charred and half-destroyed.

I jumped off the second drone and used my cybernetic leg to push it into the third, and they crashed in a glorious explosion.

"Looks like you need to call more drones," Xree said as she worked on the computer. "Our little friend won't stay down."

"Don't worry about her. It's not like she can get through the forcefield."

That was where she was wrong. She didn't know that I had a matter disrupter in my rucksack. I reached behind me and pulled it out. I used my nanites to calibrate the frequency of the shield and then let the ensuing quake create a small gap in the shield for me to rush through.

Mouse literally laughed when she saw me sneak through the bubble. "You are full of surprises."

"Why are you doing this?" I shouted. "None of this makes any sense."

"Do you really want to know who put a hit out on your father?" Xree asked as she worked.

"I think I figured out it was the two of you."

Xree laughed. "Not quite, but that's a good guess, given the circumstances."

Mouse stepped forward. "It was The Spike, Skritch. They ordered the hit on him."

"No," I replied. "That's impossible."

"I wish it were," Xree said. "But he found out we were blackmailing the corporations we infiltrated to keep our organization afloat. He was about to turn us in, so we had to act."

"Blackmailing...wait. Dotty was allowing these terrible corporations to stay in business as long as they paid you?"

"Bingo. Why do you think none of these corporations ever shut down?" Xree nodded. "It's actually something we learned from your dad, with how he kept Gilles at bay with his own self-destruct button. Dotty thought it was a fabulous idea."

I looked back at the dying Dotty. "Then why kill them?"

Mouse stepped forward. "I wasn't lying when I said I wanted to leave this city, but I needed money and a cover story to slip out unnoticed. Xree tried to talk to Dotty, but they wouldn't help us. In fact, they vowed to make sure we couldn't leave. Can you believe that? After all Neruda did for them over the years."

"We didn't have much of a choice," Xree said, finishing her typing. "I got it."

"Of course there's a choice!" I screamed. "There's always a choice."

"Do you really mourn her after finding out what she did to your father? I thought you would be on our side once you heard what we were doing and why. You got your revenge, Skritch. The Spike is no more."

"And yet you're still trying to kill me."

"You don't have to die," Mouse said. "If I wanted you dead, I would have shot you a million times by now. We were testing you this whole time."

"It's true. You're useful in a pinch. We can use that where we're going." Xree pulled out a hard drive and spun around. "Come with us, and you'll truly be free."

I took a breath to control my rage. "You killed my father and expect me to go with you?" I was angrier than I'd been in my entire life.

"I just pulled the trigger. The Spike killed your father."

"And why didn't you stop it?" I asked Xree. "No, you are as bad as they were. You revel in death. There's no way I'm going with you, and you won't get out of this building alive either."

"Then I'll have to kill you," Mouse said.

"You might…but I won't die without taking you with me."

"Get out of here," Mouse said to Xree. "I'll take care of her and be right behind you."

I tried to use my whip on Xree, but Mouse slashed through the nanites, and they fell inert on the ground. "Pretty nice trick, huh? I had this made especially for Dotty, but it will work for your nanites, too."

Xree pressed a button on the console, and the shield dropped. As it did, five more drones rushed into the room, and Xree was able to escape my grasp as I worked to avoid the laser beams of the drones.

"Last chance," Mouse said as she squared up to me, surrounded by her drones. "This place will collapse into the ground soon, and I'd rather not destroy something as beautiful as you, as the way you move through the world. You should take this as a compliment. I usually don't give people a first chance, let alone a second one. I know you're hurt and angry, but don't make a rash decision."

"Like killing the whole of The Spike?" I growled. "You slaughtered them all. They weren't all monsters. I'll bet most of them had no idea what Dotty ordered."

"You should be thanking us! Wasn't this about your revenge? Dotty ordered the hit on your father, and we killed her for you. You can walk away clear-headed and without having murder on your hand."

"Oh, there will be murder on my hands, but only because I'm going to kill you. Dotty may have ordered the hit, but you pulled the trigger."

"So be it," Mouse replied. "Remember I gave you a chance while you're bleeding out on the ground, begging for me to spare you."

CHAPTER 42

I needed to get that bracelet off Mouse's wrist if I stood any chance of killing her. The drones started to fire around the room, and I leaped forward to the one place I knew they would never attack: Mouse's position.

"See, you're learning," Mouse said, blocking my claw with her wrist. My hope was she would instinctively pull up the hand with the bracer on it, but she went the other way, which left me clawing at a metal bracer that had no strategic advantage.

I had fought Mouse two other times and learned from them that, as much as she postured, she relied too heavily on her drones to do the messy work. Sure enough, she slid away and gave her drones the ability to fire at me. I rolled away and took shelter under the command console, which was torn apart by the laser beams in a matter of seconds.

Luckily, the drones needed to recharge their weapons often, which gave me the opportunity to lurch from my position and toss the largest piece of debris I could carry at the drones, hitting one right in the big red eye in the center of their chassis, and sending it to the floor.

It didn't matter if I destroyed these drones; Mouse would bring more until I was too tired or exhausted from inhaling the black smoke to continue, then, it would be over for me. I needed to go on the offensive, so after the next onslaught of the drone's weapons, I rushed through the room and slid toward Mouse, rearing up at the last second to leap toward her, smashing her in the jaw.

She stumbled backward as I slashed at her wrist, making it bleed before she threw me across the room and left me tumbling toward Dotty's mutilated body. I crashed into it and ended up behind it when we finished our tangled tumble.

"Mouse has taken your nanites," Dotty said slowly, her eyes blinking different colors as if she were cycling through every amount of her available memory. "Use mine."

Dotty opened her chest, and a swarm of nanites rushed around my head, just as they had in Gilles's lair. I performed the incantation, and a moment later, they blinked blue, allowing me to manipulate them.

"Why are you helping me after you tried to kill me?"

"Not you...him...I am sorry for it. Logically, it was the best choice."

"Yeah, well, your logic sucks."

"Confirmed." Her voice slowed and sputtered as she said the word until the light left her eyes, and she fell inert.

I heard the drones whirling up their guns again, and I did the only thing I could think of, which was to use Dotty as a barrier for as much as her porcelain was worth. I picked up the top half of her body and rushed forward. I couldn't have done it with a metal construct, but the lightweight of their body made it possible to carry it.

As the lasers cut off pieces of the body, I kicked it forward. The drones followed Dotty's body as I remembered the sword she made out of her nanites. I ran across the room as the drones were firing on what was left of Dotty.

Mouse was not ready for my offensive, and the smirk on her face fell as I sliced her arm clean through at the elbow, and the bracer dropped to the ground with the lower half of her arm. As it clinked to the ground, the drones stopped firing.

I kicked her in the chest, and she stumbled backward. I used the momentum to grab her arm and shake the bracelet off of it.

"You little jerk!" she growled. "I'll make you pay for that."

I pressed a couple of buttons, and the drones moved in different directions. Mouse gaped, realizing that I had no control over her drones and that if she got control back from me, then she could end this once and for all.

She pulled a sword from her back and swung it erratically. Gone was the confident killer I had met before. Her eyes were out for blood now, and her bloodlust would not be satiated until she skewered me.

Mouse moved fast, but I countered every move. Without her drones, she was not as fast as me. She used them as a crutch to make her look more powerful than she was.

"Give it back," she shouted, slashing forward.

I dodged right and then left, careful not to press anything on the bracelet and get myself shot. However, the ground was quickly crumpling under me, and soon, the building would collapse and bury me inside. I had to end this before then.

Mouse slashed wide and then again, giving me a clear shot at her chest. I never killed anyone before, but I did not hesitate to stick my nanite blade into her chest. She let out a gasp as she stumbled to the ground. Her breath became labored, and she gasped as she grabbed at her chest. Then, her eyes grew wide as she reached out to me and then rolled over, dead.

There was no satisfaction in the win. Mouse had taken everything from me, and even her death left me nothing but hollow inside.

But there was still work to do. I needed to reach Xree before she could escape with all the data on Dotty's computer. I looked up at the drones and had a plan, but it required a precision strike, which was beyond my ability. I had only used one drone before and crashed it into the ground almost immediately. I would need all of them if I had any chance of stopping Xree.

I needed help. I rushed forward and found Mouse's communicator. I pressed it, hoping to remember my cousin's number.

"Who dis?" Ballister's voice shouted.

"Ballister!" I shouted. "It's Skritch. Hey, quick question. Do you know how to program a drone?"

"Of course, cuz. What kind of mechanic do you think I am?"

"The best, Ballister," I replied. "You two are the absolute best. Okay, walk me through it, and make it snappy. I don't have much time."

CHAPTER 43

I loved having tech-savvy cousins. They quickly hacked into the drones with the help of my nanites and programmed them to work with the rest of my tech. When I did, I got access to the rest of their network and found there were ten more waiting on standby a few blocks from the building.

Within five minutes, I exploded out of the front on a drone, just as the building collapsed behind me, along with everything my father believed in...or so I thought.

Now, the Spike had been destroyed, and I had killed Mouse. All that remained was to take care of Xree and recover whatever information she had taken.

"She's probably masking her car, so look for the absence of information, and you should be able to find her."

"That doesn't make any—that's not how it wo— Oh," Node said, exasperated. "Actually, I see something odd about three miles away, and it seems to be moving fast toward the center of the city."

"Then that's where I'm going," I said. "Tell me when I'm close."

I clasped onto the drone's chassis and willed it to move faster. My cybernetic arm and leg held on tightly as I could barely keep the rest of my body connected to the drone. Still, it weaved through cars even faster than I could will it, gliding between them, inches from crashing each time.

"You're closing in," Node said after a few minutes. "You're not going to believe this, but I think she's headed to Gensys."

That made complete sense. Interplanetary companies like Gensys would kill to have information on their competition, and they would pay top dollar to somebody who could provide it; the type of money that would get somebody off-planet and revered as a god anywhere in the galaxy.

"Look down and to your left. Do you see the car?" Ballister said. "Should be a hundred feet under your position."

I cocked my head down as the drone slowed enough for me to get a good grip through the wind. It took me a minute, but eventually, I found her beat-up car beneath me, weaving through cars like a reckless banshee.

"Got her," I said, redirecting the drone.

I stood on the drone as I pressed the other drones into action, or what remained of them. I had done a good job destroying them, and the building collapse cleaned up many of the others, but there was still a small cadre I could call into action.

The drone lined up on a collision course with the car as it neared Gensys. As it closed in, I activated its lasers and leaped off onto another drone that came up behind me. The first drone crashed into the back of the car, and the explosion lit it on fire. Smoke billowed out of the vehicle as it skittered out of the air. I followed it to the ground as it smashed into a pile of trash and came to a dead stop.

I waited for Xree to emerge, and when she didn't after a minute, I rushed forward and used the drones to pull her clear of the fire just as the car exploded. She was dazed and confused by the crash, and blood dripped from her forehead. Still, she held the hard drive tight.

"Was it worth it?" I asked. "All of this?"

"You expect me to say no," Xree said. "But you have clearly never been in love."

"I loved my father, and you killed him."

"I had nothing to do with that," Xree said. "This was a crime of opportunity. I saw a possible angle to save a girl I have loved since I could remember and rescue her from a crappy life. I took it, and no, I don't regret that one bit."

"Framing it like that forgives lots of deaths and millions in property damage?"

She shrugged. "We're all the heroes of our own story, aren't we?"

There was a long silence. "Mouse is dead. The Spike has been destroyed." I listened for the police cruisers in the distance. "And you're going to jail. All of this was for nothing."

She hugged the hard drive. "I still have every bit of incriminating data on fifty criminal enterprises and legit ones masking their criminality deep under the surface. I think I'll be okay."

I nodded, and seven drones appeared around me, each of them spinning up their guns. "Give me the drive, and I'll let you live."

She thought for a moment. The noble thing would have been to die for her beliefs, but she didn't have any. After a few seconds of the police cruisers getting closer, she handed over the hard drive.

"You are ice cold, Skritch. Did you know that?"

"You made me that way. All of you." I placed the drive on one of the drones and climbed on board. "Admit that you set me up when the police get here, or believe me: I will find you in jail, and I won't be so kind next time."

"You wouldn't—"

"Not me." I patted the hard drive. "But I have friends in high places. I'll be watching. The minute I stop being a wanted criminal, you'll be free to live the rest of your terrible life behind bars."

"And if I would rather die?" she asked, blood staining her mouth.

"That's your choice," I replied, rising into the air. "But I don't think you'll like what you find beyond the pale any more than here, but at least here you can atone for your sins. I hope you do."

The red and blue of the police cruisers lit the street, and I shot up through the air as they finished their final descent to the accident.

I brought the hard drive to Doug and told him to leverage it any way he could to save his family. He was quite surprised to see me commanding seven drones, but he didn't ask questions. I always appreciated that about Doug. He knew about Mouse and was a smart one, so he could put two and two together.

"The only thing I ask," I said, "is that no good people get exposed."

"Do you really think there are good people in this city?" Doug asked.

"You are," I replied. "So yes."

He shook his head. "I'm not sure after all I've done, who I've worked for, that's true, but I appreciate it all the same. I'll make sure this doesn't fall into the wrong hands and keep you safe."

I appreciated the sentiment, but Gilles would handle that since they would go down hard if I were ever exposed, except now I had the same dirt on the whole city.

It took four days for the warrants against me to go away, and they treated me like they didn't just try to destroy my life, but what could I do except try to move on, the best way I knew how.

I met Ballister and Node at the old garage a week after my showdown with Mouse and Xree, and together we cleaned up the shop.

"What now?" Ballister said after we were done.

"I'm not good for much, aside from crime, so I figured we can just do that."

"Aren't you sick of being the bad guy?" Node asked, taking a sip of beer.

I nodded. "I am. I think we can be everything The Spike tried to be but failed at—the good guys, keeping bad guys in check."

"And you think the three of us can do that by ourselves?"

I shook my head. "No, I don't, but I think people would pay good money for us to help them take down their enemies."

"I don't think that's really being the good guys," Ballister said. "That's just being less evil."

I shrugged. "Well, we gotta start somewhere."

AUTHOR'S NOTE

When I first conceived of Skritch, I said to my wife, "Well, that book's going to sell a billion copies".

Who doesn't like a cybernetic, talking, angry, magical, cat-like creature seeking revenge? All I had to do was make sure I wrote a story as epic as their origin, which took some doing. Originally, this was written for a publisher that canceled my contract less than a month before they were going to launch. Luckily, they told me I could do whatever I wanted with it, and honestly, I wanted this little furball to get out into the world. Heck, I think I could write a hundred Skritch adventures, honestly, just like I could probably write Rocket Raccoon for a billion years.

Originally, Gensys was supposed to be the big bad guy of this piece, with Jammer having worked for them in the past, and The Spike was going to be the good guy, helping Skritch finally beat Gensys and bringing them down. However, when I got into it and realized the story was a mystery, The Spike being the "bad guy" made more sense. Of course, I don't think anyone is really a good guy or a bad guy in cyberpunk. They are all just different shades of gray.

All of the characters have their motivations and think they are doing the right thing for them, even if it means justifying murder or thieving. RPGs allow us to access our moral compass and send it wildly out of tune. I doubt most of us would steal corporate secrets in real life, but it's fun to pretend. I wanted this book to inhabit that same spirit, and I hope you enjoyed it. I know I enjoyed writing it.

ALSO BY RUSSELL NOHELTY

THE OBSIDIAN SPINDLE SAGA

The Sleeping Beauty

The Wicked Witch

The Fairy Queen

The Red Rider

THE GODVERSE CHRONICLES

And Death Followed Behind Her

And Doom Followed Behind Her

And Ruin Followed Behind Her

And Hell Followed Behind Her

And Conquest Followed Behind Them

And Darkness Followed Behind Her

And Chaos Followed Behind Them

Katrina Hates the Dead

Pixie Dust

OTHER NOVEL WORK

My Father Didn't Kill Himself

Sorry for Existing

Gumshoes: The Case of Madison's Father

The Invasion Saga

The Vessel

Worst Thing in the Universe

The Void Calls Us Home

The Marked Ones

OTHER ILLUSTRATED WORK

The Little Bird and the Little Worm

Ichabod Jones: Monster Hunter

Gherkin Boy

www.russellnohelty.com